THE INTRUDERS

THE INTRUDERS

Kirk Winkler

Walker and Company
New York

First published in the United States of America in 1988 by the
Walker Publishing Company, Inc.

Published simultaneously in Canada by Thomas Allen & Son
Canada, Limited, Markham, Ontario.

Library of Congress Cataloging-in-Publication Data

Winkler, Kirk, 1948–
    The intruders.

    I. Title.
PS3573.I53224I5   1988   813'.54   88-5732
ISBN 0-8027-4084-7

Printed in the United States of America

10 9 8 7 6 5 4 3 2 1

For Arlene

Her encouragement and patience make all things possible.

THE INTRUDERS

CHAPTER 1

SHE sensed his approach long before she saw him. Perhaps it was the faint, dusty haze rising from the gray mesa to the south of her place, smearing across the wedge of blue-white summer sky. Or, perhaps, it was just her woman's way—the certain knowledge she sometimes had of coming events, a knowledge born both of intuition and necessity.

Cora Diemert squinted against the brightness and scanned the dull tableland. Weariness crept up inside her, insidious and unbidden, adding its almost unbearable weight to her limbs. She managed to shrug it off as she had done many other times: now was not the time for weakness.

"Joe, run get the shotgun," she said quietly, calmly.

The boy, just then carrying a load of mesquite into the house, stopped and looked at his mother. Immediately, he caught her urgency—less from her words than from the mannish way she stood in the yard, her bony hands on her hips and her feet spread wide apart. He had been studying her closely lately; his growing curiosity was due partly to the fact that he was almost eleven, and partly because he knew she was shouldering so much of the burden alone.

"Go get the shotgun, boy," she said again, and she meant it. This time he dropped the wood and obeyed.

In spite of her own foreboding, Cora took pleasure from knowing that he did as he was told without asking troublesome questions. Obedience was a good trait in this youngster.

Somewhere beyond the outbuildings behind her, the scrawny bull that Henry Diemert had hoped to use to seed a prize beef herd bellowed, and the weathering windmill groaned in the hot June wind. She heard them both but paid

1

no mind: the rider's imminent approach took all of her concentration. Her big hands knotted into fists while she waited for Joe to bring the gun.

Cora Diemert squinted harder at the trailing dust in the air and stood her ground.

The boy came out and handed her the gun. She felt the heft of it and fingered the heavy curved hammers. The blued steel was cool to the touch and vastly comforting. She started to cock both barrels but decided to wait until the intruder actually arrived. Past experience had taught her that just seeing her cock the weapon could discourage the faint of heart.

"Ma, who is it?" the boy asked at last. "Is it the bank man again?" His face mirrored her own, and he narrowed his eyes to slits like hers, though the skin was too supple to pull off the determined, flinty look.

"Just havin' visitors. Don't know who. Now go gather up the girls and take them inside, son."

"Is it the cowboys, Ma?" He couldn't hide the edge of real fear in his voice, no matter how hard he tried to sound old and strong.

"Just get the girls."

"Nettie's inside already. Lydie's out back weeding the garden, like you told her."

"Then get her, Joe. Now!"

"Yes, Ma." He hurried away to do her bidding, but not without looking back over his shoulder toward his mother and the tableland beyond.

She tried to visualize who it was that was coming toward her place, but this time her intuition failed her. Perhaps the cowboys. Perhaps not. The only certainty was that it wasn't good. Nothing good ever came down the trail from Fort Sumner.

Of course, it could be the banker from Las Vegas making the circuit to check on his investments, especially this particular investment of two hundred dollars cash money laid down in exchange for Henry Diemert's promissory note. They'd borrowed two hundred dollars to start a herd and buy some lumber and dig a deep well, using their whole claim as the collateral. If it was the banker, she could handle him. She had handled him before.

But the cowboys, the hired men from the big ranches . . .

At last, after what seemed like a very long time, she was able to tell for sure that it wasn't the cowboys. There was too little dust. This was a lone rider.

She inhaled deeply and realized then that she had been holding her breath, tensing for the fight. Now, perhaps, there was a reprieve. The cowboys came three or four together, all boastful and rough, but cowards underneath. And normally they came down from the north, across the flats beyond the Canadian River, all bold as brass to scare a body with their coming. This rider was bound from the south or east, perhaps from Santa Rosa or Sumner or even farther on down in the Pecos country, and he was coming along the same road Henry had taken when he'd gone off for his precious seed cattle—the herd now scattered along the grasslands north of the homestead.

A quarter mile off, at the lower end of the gray mesa where it petered out into the saltbush flats, she saw him. And he saw her. He reined in his horse and sat there.

She squinted hard. He seemed to be rolling a smoke or maybe just studying her and the layout of her place.

"Eyeing me, same as I'm eyeing him," she said out loud. "Joe! You children stay put in the house, hear?"

"Yes'm," the boy said, and she heard the door go shut and the latchstring slide over the wood as he pulled it inside. He was a smart boy.

"Well, come on then, mister."

Even though she spoke only to herself, she was conscious that her voice was low and throaty, full of determination and pinched-off fear. She went ahead and cocked the hammers on the shotgun, then held it so she could bring it up to bear on the rider with no effort whenever he tried to make his move.

As if some unspoken understanding or invisible signal had passed between them now that she was ready, the rider spurred his horse to a canter and rode straight toward her. The dust rose again from the horse's hooves and lifted into the air and plumed away eastward where it would come to settle on the saltbush crowding the rim of the mesa.

He reined in again at the gap in the bobwire that passed for a gate onto her place. His horse, splay-legged, dropped its head and seemed to fall asleep as soon as its feet quit moving.

"Ma'am," he said softly, and he touched his leather-gloved hand to the filthy, sweat-stained hat that shielded his face from the high white sun and from her gaze.

She could make out none of his features, though the voice, even in that one word, marked him scarcely older than a boy. But there was no telling from his hat-shaded face or from his clothing: he wore layer on layer of tattered clothes in spite of the heat, and they were so caked in dust that any hint of original color was lost in the sand and alkali. He was a smallish man, and as thin as the gaunt, sore-footed dun horse he rode, but she could tell nothing else of substance about him.

"You need something, mister?" she asked crossly, and she hefted the shotgun.

"Don't mean to trouble you, ma'am. Some water for the horse would be nice. Creek yonder's dry. That the Canadian back there?"

"A branch," she said, and that was all.

"Ain't much of a river out this way, is it?" He laughed a little, only to clear his throat self-consciously when she failed to acknowledge the joke.

"Your horse is played out, mister," she said after a time. "Needs a sight more than water."

"Yes, ma'am, he does. But water'll have to do."

She shifted the weight of the shotgun in her hands again, pondering, before she relented. "The tank's out back, under the windmill. Don't let him drink too fast."

The rider chuckled again, more easily this time. "No, ma'am. I surely won't." He nudged his tired horse in the ribs and it awoke and moved off in the general direction of the water.

By this time she'd heard enough of the voice to have a picture of him, almost as good as if she'd seen his face. He was very young—much younger than she, at least—a good deal more than a boy but not yet fully a man. And from Kansas, likely, the way the words came out of him flat and hard, not soft-edged like her Missouri people, nor nasal and twangy like the folks from Oklahoma Territory and Texas who peopled this part of New Mexico. She swung around as he passed to keep the muzzle of the shotgun pointed at him.

"You're on the Diemert place," she said more loudly than was necessary. "Henry Diemert. He's away, but he'll be back soon." As soon as the words were out of her, she wished she hadn't said that last part, but there was no taking it back; she held her gaze on him the way men do when they don't want to betray their thinking.

"Ain't no need for the shotgun, ma'am," he said easily.

She didn't answer.

He found the water tank and let the horse drink. Cora followed him, but she kept her distance.

"Name's Smith, ma'am. Bill Smith. On my way to Santa Fe." He sat easily in the saddle, but he didn't take his eyes off her or the big gun.

"You come from Kansas."

He twitched and scratched idly at his neck without responding.

"Well, you want water for yourself, go ahead. River's dry this time of year, like you said. Not much water at all till you reach the foothills, so you'll want to load up."

He turned away from her only long enough to study the

outline of the mountains lying purple in the west. "How far's they?"

She hesitated. "Forty miles. Maybe a little less. Santa Fe is sixty miles or so after that."

He whistled softly. "Damnation!" He slid easily from the horse and unslung the canteen from around his high Texas-style saddlehorn. The cap came off the canteen with one quick wrench, and he dipped it into the tank. Gurgling, it filled with the cool, clear water. After he'd hung it back in place, he swept off the gray hat, plunged it into the tank, and clamped it back onto his head. The water cascaded through his hair and down over his face, streaking the accumulated alkali dust.

"Whooey, that's cold! Pardon me for wastin' it, ma'am, but a fellow gets real dry out here!"

She scowled at the impertinence, but even so, her grip on the shotgun relaxed a little. She had seen his face, and despite her inclinations to be suspicious, she decided it was a good one. He had soft eyes and a good mouth under the grime and the stubble of blondish whiskers.

"Yes, it's been a hot, dry time," she said.

He pulled the balky horse away from the tank and re-mounted. His animal grunted but didn't fight him. When he raked the ribs with his spurs once more, the beast moved reluctantly away from the water.

"Thanks to you, ma'am. You say about a hunnert miles in all?"

"Forty to the mountains and sixty or seventy beyond, if you're going to Santa Fe. Or so I'm told. I haven't been there myself."

He wiped the back of his gloved hand across his mouth. "Well, thanks again." Then he was off, circling the house and heading out through the opening in the wire. He never looked back, and at the mesa he swung the horse due west, into the wind.

She watched carefully until he was only a little speck

crossing the shallow wash Henry had named Coyote Creek. Even after he was out of sight entirely, she waited. Only when she no longer saw the traces of his dust, when her intuition told her that he had truly ridden on, did she call the children to open the door.

Lydia, the elder daughter, burst out first, her curiosity driving her as surely as a wood fire drives the steam in the kettle; the disappointment of missing a glimpse of this stranger showed plainly on her freckled face.

"Who was he, Ma?" she asked, speaking for the other two children now following her outside. Only Joe scowled at the question.

"Just a man, passing through." Cora carefully checked the gun to be sure the hammers were safely down and took it inside, to return it to its place above the old chiffonier in the corner. Then she poured herself a cup of thick boiled coffee. Her hands were shaking.

Joe, who still stood in the open doorway, watched her gulp the hot coffee, and then he, too, left her completely alone. But he didn't join his sisters in their game of hide-and-seek. Instead, he sat in the dust in the shade of the squat adobe house, his knees drawn up to his chin, trying to think this thing out.

The night came on in a blaze of brilliant reds and lavenders, and before the sun had set completely, the oppressive heat and scorched-earth smell of the day had begun to fade away.

Evening was the only time that Cora Diemert allowed herself the luxury of thinking kindly of this New Mexico wilderness where her husband had set them down. Sometimes—rarely, but sometimes—the loveliness of the evening made up for the numbing work and the hardships they faced each day. These evenings were almost always pleasant interludes between one cycle of work and the next. The supper of beans cooked in smoking lard, of corn bread with strong sage honey, and coffee boiled strong was behind them; while the girls washed the dishes and Joe carried in more of the scarce wood for the night, Cora could rest in her rocker and watch the play of colors in the sky and smell the night-softened aroma of mesquite and grama grass blown in from the river bottoms, or she could wait for the occasional tan mule-deer doe to step out of the shadows of the mesa and sniff the air. Even the bickering of eight-year-old Lydia and six-year-old Nettie was comforting in this twilight hour, for their little-girl arguments confirmed for Cora the certainty that life really did go on, that childhood and its joys could exist and flourish in such a remote place. After such hardships, that was nothing short of a miracle.

The brace of old oxen lowed plaintively, as if her own melancholy had somehow settled on them. She should get rid of them; all they did was eat the grass in her pasture. They had lived out their usefulness and so should be gone, but they'd been loyal for too long, had brought them all too many miles. She was glad when they quieted, leaving the girls' argument the only sound beyond the soft rustling of the night creatures in the grass.

She couldn't help but notice that Joe no longer shared in the childhood fighting; but then he was growing up, as he must. The only time she worried too much about her children was when Lydia became overly somber and sat in the corner by herself, lost in thought. Cora wished a longer, gentler childhood for her brood, especially for this elder daughter who should have a chance to grow up to be gay and beautiful and full of the fire of life. But, of course, the children were more like her than like Henry; they would be a serious lot, given to serious concerns. Which was, all things considered, the best thing for them. Henry had been Henry, and once upon a time she had loved him dearly for it, but he had brought them to this cruel place, too, and for that she could never forgive him.

For that and for dying.

The summer stars came out, and the sliver of moon and the bright evening star rose together over the mesa. A long way off a coyote began to howl, and others even farther off in the open loneliness of the desert answered him.

She took a lantern from the house and went out back to check on the livestock. What was left of the herd, which had been Henry's dream, was beyond her view, out on the high open grasslands, unattended and uncounted. But the living things in the yard, which had always been her responsibility, were accounted for each evening: the Rhode Island Red hens and the rooster already asleep in the little coop at one end of the shed; the oxen, belching and chewing their cuds in the pasture; the mules, brushed down and turned in for the night with a handful of oats as a reward for their labors in the garden.

The swaybacked old milch cow, even older than the oxen, was still awake this late in the evening, as if she was having trouble sleeping with the advancing of the years. The cow lowed softly at her approach, and Cora patted its broad tan flank. The cow was going dry. Off her feed, Henry had said toward the last, but Cora had always known better. The old girl was tuckered out. A calf or two too many, some born on the long walk all the way from Missouri to New Mexico, and always giving milk to the family had taken a heavy toll. Now she had only tough grass and weeds to browse and a young-blooded bull, properly the sire of beef cattle, waiting to mount her when it was her season. There would likely never be another season. She was getting ready to die. It would be a quiet death when it came, and in a way sadder than the sudden, violent ending to life that was becoming all too familiar to Cora.

She heard the bull snuffling in his pen and left him alone. She hated the bull. To her, he was the symbol of their sorrow and their failure. He'd done his duty, as Henry had put it, but then his half-wild mates had wandered off into the wilderness to bear their young.

With her rounds completed, she turned her steps for the house. She heard the gentle rustling of the fat round leaves of the single old cottonwood by the water tank, but there was nothing there that needed looking after. At least not tonight. Perhaps tomorrow, if she were in a better mood, if the black dread that the stranger's coming had aroused in her had vanished, she might find a solitary moment to sit in the shade of that tree. But not now. Not when, from somewhere deep within her, she still felt strange eyes upon her. Still, she paused to enjoy the night air a moment longer.

Inside, the children would be readying for bed.

Dearest Lord, she thought, I wish I had proper beds for them; the kind with a decent ticking stuffed to the point of hardness with horsehair, the sort of bed they'd left behind in Missouri. Here she had only cornshucks, and old and broken-down ones at that. She remembered her mother's beautiful feather bed, and it made her want to weep, though of course she would not.

How she missed Missouri, especially on nights like this when the coming of a stranger stirred so much anxiety within her, both because she feared strangers and because she hated having to drive away human companionship at the point of a shotgun. Missouri hadn't been like that. The Galts and the Eberhards, the Sawyers and Henrichs and Diemerts had all shared their little hollow at the very northern end of the Ozarks, and it had been a good enough life for all of them. Cora was a Galt herself, and although her parents were long since dead, she'd always taken great pleasure in her family, in having her sisters and brothers and their broods come by for pork roast and apple pie in the autumn when the slaughtering was done and the crops were in, or even just for cornbread and molasses in the leaner times. Many years they'd all lived hand-to-mouth, especially right after the war; but even in those days life had never been frightening there, in one's home place, among one's own people.

The trouble was that Missouri hadn't been enough for Henry. He'd always been a wild one, needing excitement, something her folks had cautioned her about more than once. He'd tried to enlist in John Charles Fremont's Union Army when he was barely thirteen, and after the war he'd been to Little Rock and St. Louis just to see the sights. So a tiny Missouri valley nestled among the chopped-off hills had held little thrill for him.

Through their early years together, he'd been a wild man who needed an understanding woman; then, when age should have begun to settle him a little, he'd taken to scheming over grand adventures that he made up in his head. She'd put her foot down, of course. There would be no adventuring, no leaving the home place. And he'd abided by her wishes, at least until their eldest—Henry, Junior—had died of the scarlet fever. By rights, the little grave should have been all the more reason for staying, but she'd felt like running, too, if only from the hurt of losing her little boy. So when Henry had told her of the new lands opening up in the Indian Territory, lands free for the taking, she'd assented.

A new land, with a new chance to make something of themselves, she'd thought. Perhaps that would be all right. But once Henry got himself on the move, the Indian Territory hadn't been enough. Oh, he'd been content enough for a time, while everything was still new and exciting, but when the newness had faded, he'd have nothing but that they move on again, first to the Panhandle, that no man's land, and then on again into the new territory, this New Mexico. She'd railed and cried out against it, but in the end, when he'd decided to go, she could do nothing but follow.

And so now here she was, in this short-grass country where the only trees were the scattering of creek-bed cottonwoods and mesquite, and only the saltbush and prickly pear kept the sand from blowing away in the restless winds. Not at all like the box elders and pin oaks and fall red sumacs of home.

Yes, by rights, the little grave left behind in Missouri *should* have been enough reason to stay.

By that logic, of course . . .

She shook her head and refused to look at the cottonwood and the pile of stones beneath it, refused the thought of them binding her to this place.

The last light of day was long past spent. The night things, the June bugs and crickets and long-tailed mice and fluttering bats, were coming into their domain. It was time for sleeping, time for huddling against the unknown until daylight would come and give her a larger measure of courage once more.

Cora went inside. She tucked the children in and pulled the faded comforters around them to ward off the night chills. No matter how hot it got in the daytime, the nights here were cold, and no matter how much of the precious wood she burned, the chill never left until the morning sun had returned.

"Ma?" Lydia said after prayers.

"Yes?"

"I think the sweet corn's dying, but the squash is coming along real good."

She kissed the girl on the forehead. "At least we'll have something then, won't we?"

"Ma?"

"Hush now, Lydie. It's time to sleep."

"But Ma, read to me from the Bible."

"Tomorrow night. You children need your rest now."

Still, it was a good idea; a comforting one, Cora thought. She lowered the flame in the lantern and settled into her rocker and opened the Bible so she might read to herself by what little light remained.

The book came open easily to the Psalms, her favorite part. Although some of the language was difficult for her to understand, she loved the sounds of the words and the rhythms of them when she read them aloud, and always there was enough meaning to linger over, to ponder in the soft stillness of another lonely night.

Her eyes fell on Psalm 102:

> Hear my prayer, O Lord, and let my cry come unto thee. Hide not thy face from me in the day when I am in trouble; incline thine ear unto me: in the day when I call answer me speedily.

It was at that moment that she heard the crisp report of the carbine.

CHAPTER 2

HE'D spotted the grave as soon as he'd rounded the house and headed for the watering tank. She'd tried to hide it, but even so she'd had to pile enough stones around the grave to discourage the coyotes, and weeds had crept into the edges of the sod where it had been broken by the spade. The grave had made him nervous, more nervous than her belligerent ways, more nervous even than the cocked shotgun. A woman with a man was predictable, even if that man was away, as she'd said; but a woman with her man dead—and, he guessed, buried by her own hand—was something else again: as unpredictable as an April storm, and certainly as dangerous. He was glad to be shed of her, no matter how badly he needed some rest and a square meal and a place to keep a lookout for the one he knew was following.

Still, the water alone had been a godsend. The high plains country was a blank, forbidding land this time of year, and the main rivers like the Canadian were as dry as the little arroyos between the mesas. Even if a man and horse found water, it was likely to be stinking with alkali. Nor was his map much help. He'd never been in this region before, had never seen so much nothingness. Even the flats of western Kansas were hospitable by comparison. There, at least, a body knew the land would stay unchanged for mile after mile, but here the face of the plains had a way of changing abruptly, and even with the map, even with some assurance that he was following the correct trail, he felt lost. Being pushed and pursued had added a touch of panic, too, so that the valleys that engulfed him and the flat mesas, rising as they did almost straight up from the desert floor, seemed sinister and made him feel puny and alone. So, to have seen the tumbledown ranch where he knew his pursuer would not be, to have smelled and tasted sweet water, and to have heard a human voice had seemed at the start of it to be too good to be true.

Of course, the horse had smelled the water first, and he reckoned that he couldn't have avoided the ranch or the woman even if he'd tried. The horse was going there to get a bellyful of water, regardless.

The horse was a good one, or had been once, but it was probably too late in the game for it to be much good ever again. He slapped at the scrawny back, and white alkali dust billowed out of the lusterless hair. The dun twisted one ear but didn't raise its head.

Played out for sure. Wasn't that what the woman had said? Well, she wasn't far wrong. He'd have to get a fresh mount for himself before very long. Maybe at Las Vegas, if he could get the critter up into the mountains ahead.

He pulled the map out of his coat pocket and unfolded it carefully. The creases had worn the paper through. Turning it around so the sun would play on the faded lettering, he found what he was after: Las Vegas, New Mexico, and between here and there the towns of Springer and Wagon Mound, both on this side of the mountains. Almost unconsciously, he raked his spurs over the horse's ribs, nudging it westward just a little faster, just to keep ahead of the one who was coming after.

The woman would tell his pursuer about Santa Fe, but that probably wouldn't fool him. Not for a minute.

Maybe, the young man thought, I can find a spot up in the mountains, somewhere with a little good grass for the horse, and just lay up and wait for him and get it over with once and for all.

The wind tugged at his hat, and he snugged up the chin strap. The day was going all white from swirling windblown dust and the brilliance of the sun. Together, the wind and the sun were doing their level best to suck him dry, trying to leave him as empty and fragile as a November corn husk. He could almost feel the refreshing water from the woman's place being sucked out of him.

They moved slowly up a little valley between two mesas, the horse taking on a slow, rolling gait that was the best the sore-footed beast could muster now that they were beginning the long slow climb toward the mountains.

After a while, the man tried to roll a cigaret, but the wind blew the makings away.

"Probably just as well. Parch my throat, anyhow," he said aloud, and he reached for his canteen.

It was while his head was tilted back to take a long, cool swig of the water that it happened.

The horse balked and sidestepped, and he fell backward out of the saddle, landing hard. The dun whinnied and kicked at him and half turned and loped away. He could see its eyes rolling, the whites showing.

"Damn you, hoss!" he shouted at the top of his lungs as he picked himself up and moved his limbs, making sure nothing was broken. And then he saw the reason the horse had thrown him.

The snake.

It was a big rattler, gray with dark crosshatchings, seven feet long and as thick as a grown man's forearm. He scrambled to his feet and the snake coiled again, warning him with the sharp buzz of the rattle that he hadn't heard until now. The black forked tongue darted at him, and the triangular evil head rose well above the massed coils as if measuring the distance between the man and itself for the quick thrust.

He groped in the waistband of his trousers for the old Colt's revolver.

There wasn't time. The snake struck hard, lashing out half the length of the heavy gray body with amazing swiftness. The man stepped back, and now his own reflexes took charge. The snake's fangs found only sand, and before it could coil up again, the thick leather of his riding boot came down across its neck, leaving the head sticking out one side of the sole and the twisting body out the other. The man put all his weight down on that foot; the snake whipped from side to side, struggling to free itself.

At last he found the revolver, drew and cocked it, and blew the snake's head away. The heavy body jerked once, and then the rattles stilled.

The little thrill of killing gave him a twinge of gooseflesh at the nape of his neck, and he smiled.

"Damn snake," he said. "Teach you to mess with me." Then he looked around quickly to assure himself that the rattler had no brethren lurking about. Satisfied, he picked up the long body by the tail and snapped off the rattles for a souvenir. Only then did he pay any attention to the horse. The dun had bolted again at the sound of the gunshot, and now it stood twenty yards off, its sides heaving as if it had just finished a hard gallop. When he approached, the horse flared its nostrils and rolled its eyes and sidestepped away from him.

In just that little movement, he could tell what had happened. From the way the horse favored its right foreleg, he saw all that he needed to see. The snake had found a mark after all. Probably it had been out sunning itself on the warm sand, half asleep, and the horse had nearly stepped on it. Aroused, the snake had managed to strike, sinking those needle-sharp fangs into the horse's fetlock. That was when the dun had thrown him.

He clucked to the horse to calm it down so he could come close enough to get a good look at the bite.

There it was, all right. Almost invisible in the dirty gray-brown hair. Two small spots, just pinpricks, and not even oozing blood. But the flesh was already swelling. He tried to take the horse's leg in his hands, but it shied again.

He looked back at the snake. It was a damn big one, that

was for sure, and the horse was almost played out, anyhow. A healthy horse might pull through, but now . . .

He clucked again and moved close to the horse. The bite had been solid, one fang mark right over a vein bulging beneath the hide. The worn horse whinnied again and blew hard through its nose, already struggling to breathe.

"He killed you, hoss," he said softly. "Be damned if he didn't." He crooned an old trail song and patted the horse's neck to calm it. In a little bit the horse had quieted enough for him to strip off the saddle, the carbine in its long leather boot, the bedroll, and the precious saddlebags. Then he slipped off the dirty saddle blanket and the harness and scratched at the horse's long, tattered ear. The wheezing was getting worse.

"Should of give you a name a long time ago, hoss. You carried me a far piece, and all I did was get you killed."

He put his gear down near the dead snake and regarded the horse. It was truly amazing that such a small amount of poison—not more than a few drops, surely—could kill something so big, so quickly.

Maybe the horse would recover, pass the crisis with a little rest.

The animal shuddered and stamped its feet as it struggled.

After a time, he pulled his carbine out of the boot and sighted along the blued steel barrel, aiming directly between the horse's brown eyes.

He levered a shell into the chamber and sighted again. "I got you killed, and you left me afoot forty miles from nowhere. Guess that's an even trade, hoss."

He pulled the trigger. The dun's forelegs jerked and stiffened, then it shuddered, crumpled over, and died. This time, there was no enjoyment in the killing for him.

He rolled a smoke and rested on the saddle, considering the possibilities. According to the woman's reckoning, it was a full thirty-five miles and more just to the mountains, and a man couldn't hope to make that climb afoot dragging heavy leather and his guns. There were a couple of towns nestled in the foothills, and a man on horseback might get there tomorrow sometime, take a late supper in the cantina, put up for a few hours in whatever passed for a hotel, and be gone without saying a dozen words to anyone. But a man afoot . . . well, if he ever got there at all . . .

The one following him might likely beat him there and be waiting, ready to have it out. It was a chance he couldn't afford to take.

So maybe he could steal a horse.

Hell, he hadn't seen a loose saddle horse in eighty miles, and how the hell was he supposed to catch one on foot, anyway?

There was the woman, of course.

He rolled up the rifle scabbard and tied it and the heavy saddlebags to the saddle horn with a short piece of rope. The blanket he'd leave, but he'd bury it in the sand to hide it.

Stupid, he thought. A dead horse will be a hell of a lot easier to find than a blanket, but he couldn't bury the horse. Maybe, with a little luck, the vultures would take care of it before anyone came along to discover what had happened.

He hoisted the heavy saddle onto his back, held it in place with his left hand, and picked up the rifle in his right. It was plenty enough load for a man to carry, but there wasn't a thing he could do about it. He considered leaving the saddle, but the woman had mules, and he had no intention of riding a mule bareback.

He took a last look at the mountains, then set off down the way he'd come. Back to the woman's place. It was four, maybe five miles, and he'd not reach it until well past dark, but at least he knew the way. He'd be able to carry his truck that far. And in the meantime, he'd try not to think about her shotgun.

The going was hard through the sand and grama, and for once he wished he weren't wearing the high, block-heeled boots. They'd been handed down from his eldest brother and had no shape at all anymore. The soles were thin, and they were at least one size too big. He cursed again, but this time it was at nothing in particular. Unlike the horse and the snake, there really wasn't anyone to blame for the boots.

At least now the wind was at his back, pushing him on instead of filling his face with dust. The sweat trickled out of his hair and onto his forehead. He licked his lips, and they were salty.

The country seemed to swallow him up now that he was a part of it, with the soles of his feet shielded from direct contact by only the thinnest of worn boot leather. The clumps of grama grass waved tall and blue-green in the wind. Once, he stumbled into one of the clusters of prickly pear that littered the ground, and a sharp barbed spine pierced his boot and lodged in the side of his foot. He yelped in spite of himself and dropped the saddle. It took several minutes to work the stubborn thorn out of his flesh, and by the time he did, the thing had swollen up to three times its normal thickness. He rubbed the sore foot and at the same time marvelled at the prickly pear's little act of survival: the water-starved plant was capable of sucking the fluids right out of his body. Still, his appreciation didn't make it hurt any less when he put the boot back on and resumed his hike. About all he could do was grit his teeth and try his best to forget it.

This New Mexico was damned sure bleak and foreboding. The blue vault of sky melted into the gray-green horizon that was broken only occasionally by the mesas. Heat shimmers gave the whole thing a wavy, unsettled look, as if he were seeing it all through a thin layer of rippling water. Besides the grama and the cactus, there were few plants— saltbush, mostly—and no trees except an occasional cotton-wood or mesquite in the very bottoms of the gullies where water would collect. And there were no signs of animal life, either, beyond the fierce red ants that labored so industriously around their bare sand hillocks. He avoided the ants, knowing their sting.

He remembered from all the old stories that this was cattle country, the old Goodnight-Loving trail country; but it looked damn poor at that, the sort of land his older brothers had spoken of so often, land where a man could be free if he was strong enough and willing enough to grab a big chunk of it. This land was utterly worthless for anything but cattle, or maybe sheep; and even to his unpracticed eye, it was clear that it would take a lot of acres to feed one head.

He closed his eyes to conjure up an image of the miles of waving, ripened wheat on the high Kansas plain. He'd always thought of that as a harsh land, but this was far worse. He'd been riding across it for days, but from the high vantage point of the horse's back, he hadn't really taken a hard look at it. On foot, with the feel of the land transmitted through thin sole leather with each step, he couldn't avoid looking at it, being one with it.

He measured the shadow that marched along in front of him. Ten, maybe twelve feet long now. The sun was getting low, nearly to the rim of the mountains behind him. It would be dark all too soon. He tried to get sure bearings on the horizon, attempting a guess at how far he'd come already. He stared hard at the horizon as he tried to determine whether the mesa there on the eastern edge of his visible world was the one he'd skirted just before he'd found the woman's place. He couldn't tell, wouldn't be able to until he saw the cottonwood tree or smoke from her evening cooking fire. The land spread out before him was deceiving; it looked utterly flat, but instead, it was broken into shallow washes and deep arroyos, rocky flats and undulating grasslands that had a monotonous and frightening sameness about them. Only his shadow, moving on straight in front of him, assured him that he was heading in the right direction.

He'd been lost in Kansas once, when he was a little boy. So lost in the bewildering sameness of that wheat country that he'd spent a whole night out of doors and alone, cowering in the darkness and listening for the wolves he was sure would come to devour him. Luckily, there were no wolves that night, not even coyotes, but the experience had left scars on him just the same. He hated being along at night. One man, or even a poor horse, was company enough, but to be utterly alone was torture. Almost without thinking, he checked his lengthening shadow and hurried on. Perhaps the carbine would have to do for company this night.

Or—the ugly thought could not be kept at bay—if he truly did get lost and couldn't find the woman's place, the rifle might be all the companionship he would ever have again.

He kept walking and watching. His shadow stretched out and softened and diffused into the general grayness of sand and saltbush. Still, he kept moving onward as the sky turned paler blue, then fiery red, then lavender, and finally black.

Just when the stars stood out at their coldest and whitest against the black of night, he saw the light of the little house. He saw only a glimmer of yellow lamplight at first; but after a few hundred yards, he was sure that it was her place, with the thin wisps of smoke rising from the chimney visible against the fat full moon on the horizon and the kerosene lamplight filtering yellow and warm through the heavily greased paper tacked over the window opening.

He laid the saddle down and sat on it right there on the trail and watched the house. His own loneliness dissipated into the cooling night air; no wolves would be on his trail tonight. But there was a problem. Now that the great hurdle of the open desert had been crossed, now that he had found this place of refuge, he somehow had to keep her from blasting him into Kingdom Come with that old blunderbuss of hers.

He rolled a smoke and considered.

She was a skittish woman; he'd seen that already. So he couldn't just go up and knock on the door. On the other hand, if he tried to sneak in and bed down quietly in one of the outbuildings, she or one of the children might stumble onto him come first light. Or the livestock, awakened from their slumbers, might sound an alarm that would bring her running—and shooting. None of the prospects seemed too good at the moment. He considered stealing a mule, then discarded the notion. He was no mule thief; not at night, anyway, when the thing could be counted on to bray its brains out.

"Damnation!" he said aloud, and he ground out the glowing butt of the cigaret. Immediately, he chastised himself for this habitual swearing, but it had been a bad day, the worst in a long time. The worst since that other very bad day in Kansas.

He thought of the rattler again, and the satisfaction he'd felt in blowing its head off. Too bad he hadn't seen it in time to save the horse. If he had, he'd have been well toward the mountains by now, maybe resting along some clear-water stream coming out of the pine country. Maybe he'd have been smelling the wind that would carry the sweet, smoky smells of piñon and ponderosa.

"Hell's own fire," he said under his breath, and he reached for the carbine he'd laid across the saddle horn. It took real effort to stand again; his muscles were already cramping. He dragged the saddle to the gate in front of the little house and levered a cartridge into the carbine chamber. Pointing the rifle to the sky, he pulled the trigger.

She would have fair warning. And he, protected by the blue-black shroud of night beyond the spill of lantern light, would have time to identify himself or to fire again if she came after him with her big black gun.

CHAPTER 3

SHE looked at him as he inched into the circle of yellow light, the carbine held out in front of him, the muzzle pointed toward the sky. He was talking steadily, soothingly, as she had heard Henry talk to fractious cattle when he wanted them to calm down. She kept her thumb on the hammers of the shotgun, though she knew that if he'd meant to kill her, he wouldn't have fired a warning shot.

"My horse died, ma'am. Got snakebit. Had to destroy it myself. Wasn't much of a horse, which of course you saw, but it left me afoot. Been a powerful long walk, ma'am, and I'd be much obliged if you'd allow me to put up for the night in that shed yonder. I'd gladly pay you, too. And for a bite to eat, if you have it."

"Don't have food for strangers."

"Then just a place to sleep?"

She looked at him carefully and took a better grip on the shotgun, just in case. "Why should I?"

"Christian thing to do, ma'am, I reckon. Been a hard walk, just carryin' these things. Gives me a new appreciation of my horse, I s'pose, luggin' this saddle. I could sure use a place to sleep in out of the weather."

She glared at him for a long time before she answered.

"You just sit down right there, mister. Don't come any closer. Put your saddle down and sit on it. Right there! And lay the gun by while I think."

He did as he was told.

They stared at each other across the yard. Her children had been awakened by the commotion and came to the doorway to gawk. The youngest rubbed sleep out of her eyes and hid behind her mother's gray skirt, but the older two stepped out alongside Cora and, mimicking her, gazed squarely at this stranger who had intruded upon them twice in the same day. He saw that they were very like her: tough and no-nonsense, as ready to do battle as she. They were children, certainly, but they were going to grow up awfully fast in this place; a blind man could see that. They were going to have a tough life, especially with no man around except the one he figured was buried in the grave yonder by the cottonwood.

He rolled a cigaret and sat and waited. It was good enough, after all, just to sit and rest within sight of other humans, even if they hadn't decided yet whether they were going to be the least bit friendly.

After a time she sent the two girls off to bed. She allowed the boy to stay at her side while she pondered. After a while the young man figured she must have decided that he was telling the truth about the horse. And why not? Both he and the saddle were covered with dust, and he knew that he must look nearly as blown as the horse had.

"If you'd treated that horse right, it would of had enough sense to step around a snake instead of getting bit," she said crossly, testing him.

He dragged deeply on the butt of the cigaret until the red coal nearly burned his lips, then he snuffed it out. "I guess you're on the money there, ma'am. I reckon I killed that poor nag. I surely did."

He laughed as easily as he could under the circumstances. "But hell, ma'am—beggin' your pardon, I don't mean to curse in front of the boy—I didn't mean to harm that horse. We've been riding far on short rations is all. That was an oat-fed horse, ma'am, and it didn't much take to feedin' on the tough grass hereabouts. I should have gone easier, I know, but it's a sight too late now. So I'm just askin' you for a bed tonight. When it comes to it, out of doors is all right, too. It don't have to be in one of your outbuildings or anything, though I'd ask for a little clean straw to lie on, just to take a bit of the hardness out of the ground."

"And then what will you do? In the morning, I mean?"

He took it as the first sign that she was softening. Even so, he decided against pressing his luck. "If you'll kindly let me sleep on your place, I'll worry about that in the morning. To tell the truth, I ain't thought too much about it yet. Right now, I'm just wore out."

"We've got no spare livestock to sell you. And I'd not be of a mind to sell good horseflesh to a man who abuses his animals, anyway. Even if I had the horseflesh, which I surely do not."

Her voice was still stern, but he detected the edge of rough acceptance creeping into it. He relaxed just a little. Not completely, of course; he knew it might be just his imagination, and she still kept her thumb on that pair of heavy hammers, but maybe she *was* softening a bit. Maybe she was as happy to have a grown-up human being around in the still of the night as he was.

"I ain't askin' you for anything, ma'am, beyond a place to sleep. I won't trouble you."

Slowly, she let go of the hammers, but she kept the muzzle aimed in his direction, just in case.

"There's a workshop off to the side of the chicken coop. It's a separate room to the front. Door's on the east end."

He grinned easily now that the deal was struck. "I don't mind chickens, ma'am. I don't smell too pretty myself, I s'pose."

She nodded and he noticed the faintest trace of a smile play across her lips, or maybe it was just the shadows of night playing tricks on his eyes. "Then I'll have the boy here throw down some clean straw for you."

He touched a finger to the brim of his hat. "I'm much obliged, ma'am. I truly am."

"You said your name was . . . ?"

"Smith. Bill Smith."

She cocked her head as if waiting for more, and this time there was no mistaking the frown.

"Well, Mister Smith," she said slowly, "my name's Cora Diemert. You're welcome to the straw and water. Mind you now, if I hear a single squawk out of one of my hens, I'll figure you're stealing and I'll come running." She wagged the shotgun a little. "You keep that in mind!"

"Yes, ma'am," he said, and he managed a reasonably broad smile.

And so it was decided. He sat on his saddle and smoked another cigaret while he waited for the boy she had called Joe to haul some fresh straw into the little room off the chicken coop, then he carried his own truck back there and made himself as good a bed as he could. All the while, she stood off a way, just out of the light, cradling the shotgun in her arms.

He arranged the saddle for a pillow and laid out his heavy saddlebags alongside where his head would be. The chickens, on the other side of the thin slat wall that he guessed was made from the box of an old wagon, stirred and shifted on their roosts and dropped off to sleep again, and from somewhere deep in the dirty shavings and sawdust along the adobe wall behind the grinding wheel he heard the soft rattle of a mouse. When he breathed too deeply, the pungent smell of accumulated chicken manure and grain dust made his eyes water, but he was plenty tired enough; he'd get used to it. He'd never been one to sleep under the stars whenever there was any other alternative; and if he had to smell the ammonia of chickens to be inside this night, he would do it, and gladly. The morning would come soon, and that would be time enough to dicker with the woman over the price of one of her mules.

Yessir, that could wait for morning. He laid out the blanket from his thin bedroll. It smelled vaguely of his dead horse, a comforting, familiar sort of smell against the background of the chickens.

"Mr. Smith?" she called out.

He stirred and raised himself on one elbow, his right hand already at the butt of the gun still tucked into his trousers.

"Yes, ma'am?"

"I'll have the boy bring you some cold corn bread and honey if you'd like. And there'll be bacon and coffee in the morning."

"Thank you, ma'am!"

"But don't let me hear them chickens!"

He laughed with genuine ease. "No, ma'am. I wouldn't harm a feather on their heads!"

He waited for the cornbread and wolfed it down when it came. After the boy had gone away again he tried to sleep but could not; he arose and took a night stroll around the place as quietly as he could so as not to rile the woman. He used the privy, inspected the poorly concealed grave, watched the bull for a while, and turned in again. The straw felt more comfortable now, and even the smell of the chickens seemed less bitter. He drew the saddlebags up close to him and laid the old revolver out where he could find it quickly if he were awakened.

Up at the house, the woman barred the door and made a show of getting ready for bed until she was certain that all three of her children were asleep. Then she turned the lamp down low and settled into her rocker with her favorite shawl spread across her knees and the shotgun in her lap. She would doze, but she would also listen for the sound of footsteps on the stone-hard earth or the strangled sound of a chicken being killed.

Yet, strangely, she was not uncomfortable, or even afraid. There was a man around her place again. A decent enough man, too, or so her intuition told her, even if he did abuse his horse and—perhaps—lie about his name. She would have to bargain hard when the time came, as it surely would, when he would want one of her mules. Or maybe she would rent him the buckboard and have Joe drive him to Wagon Mound. But that was crazy. Fatigue was muddling her thinking.

Then it occurred to her that he might come to realize that Henry was not just away . . .

Surely he knew that already. Any fool could tell, she supposed, and this man-boy did not appear the fool. None of the intruders were.

Even though she wished it otherwise, her thoughts turned from the stranger to the banker and then to the cowboys from the Pecos country.

A coyote howled from a long way off; and another, closer, answered.

She was glad she'd given the man shelter. Someone beholden to her, even in a small way, might come in helpful. Though of course she'd have to be careful, even of this one.

Sometime after midnight she drifted off into a fitful but dreamless sleep.

CHAPTER 4

THE big man settled heavily into the rickety wooden seat and leaned back carefully. The chair groaned under his weight but held up. He took off his black Stetson and blew off what he could of the loose gray dust and brushed up the nap of the felt before he bothered to wipe the grit off his weathered face. After all, he took great pride in the hat. It had cost him ten dollars.

The piercing blue eyes set deeply back of his hawklike nose took in the whole of the dim cantina, and he listened carefully to see if he could catch bits and pieces of the conversations going on at the other tables. Some were in Spanish, which, as always, irritated him, but he could translate enough to tell that the discussions were of everyday matters and so weren't threatening. These people had sized him up the instant he had strode inside; in their backwater way, they had decided that he was better left alone.

He mopped his face and blew his nose loudly into his bandana. Not a single head turned, though surely all had heard him.

The bartender, a withered little Mexican who probably owned the place, scurried over to him.

"*Señor?*"

"You have steaks?"

"*Sí.* That is, yes we do, *señor.*"

Then I'll have a steak. Cooked through. And potatoes if you have them."

"We have beans, *señor. Frijoles refritos.*"

"Jesus! That all? If I never see another goddamn bean it'll be too soon."

The little man smiled weakly, showing a mouthful of mossy teeth. "*Sí, señor.* It is all we have."

"All right then. Steak and beans. And black coffee and fresh bread if you have it."

The Mexican nodded and started to back away, but the hawk-nosed man reached out for him and caught him by the sleeve.

"And some information, *por favor.* You seen any strangers around here lately? *Gringos?*"

The little man's eyes flickered across the broad dark face before him and he shook his head hesitantly.

The big man saw fear in the Mexican's eyes, and he knew he'd been misunderstood. He couldn't help but chuckle, though he held it low in his throat so that no one at any of the neighboring tables could hear.

"Not me, friend. You can tell the whole goddamn world you seen me if you want. I'm looking for another *gringo.* A young man, slight of build. Would of come in from the east, most likely. Maybe today, maybe a week ago. Maybe not yet."

"I have seen no one, *señor,*" the Mexican said sincerely.

The big man sighed and dug deep in his pocket for a gold piece. He slapped it down onto the table and dropped his thick fingers over the coin so the Mexican would see only the smallest corner of the shiny metal.

"That's for whoever tells me where I can find the skinny *gringo.* Understand?"

"*Comprende, señor,*" the Mexican said, eagerly this time, the sure glint of avarice suddenly plain in his eyes. "But I have not seen him."

The big man searched the large brown eyes before him looking for deceit. Finding none, he grinned. "Okay, then get me the damned steak and beans, will you?"

Beans! He almost shuddered at the thought as he waited for his meal. Lord, why beans? He'd eaten nothing but beans and a little moldy salt pork all the way from Kansas; and then he'd hit New Mexico, where he'd found that the damned greasers had a brand new way to fix them, but they were still beans. After weeks in the saddle, it seemed to him as if he and his big bay mare were in some sort of perverse contest to see who could break wind more often.

He'd been at this thing too long, anyway, and he knew it. There had been some sign at first, then he'd lost all track of his prey out in the vastness of the Staked Plains, so he'd hurried on to Fort Sumner and sent his wires to every sheriff and constable he could reach. That way he'd picked up the trail again, with confirmation that Shingleton had been seen west of Tucumcari, heading straight into the Canadian country, the old Goodnight-Loving cow trail territory. Armed with that information, he'd ridden up from Fort Sumner as fast as the bay could take him, hoping to intercept his quarry before the kid crossed over the Sangre de Cristos and made the quick, straight dive toward Colorado—assuming the kid still hoped to rendezvous with the others—or turned down the Rio Grande toward Juarez and real freedom. If young Shingleton had enough of a fresh start, and if he headed south toward Mexico . . . well, that would be the end of it.

Then there would be no way to avoid wiring Ben Comstock in El Paso to take over the chase. Of course, even if the kid went north, he should telegraph old Arnold Toothacker in Pueblo. A cautious man would do it now, but the hawk-nosed man hated Ben Comstock—hated sharing the chase and the glory of the capture—even more than he hated Shingleton. And Toothacker, the old alcoholic, was beneath contempt, the laughingstock of the Federal Marshal Service. So it was best to hope that something turned up here in Wagon Mound, where there was room to work without calling in such "help" as those two would provide.

The steak came. It was blood-rare and so freshly killed that it was all he could do to chew it. The only saving graces were that it wasn't moldy and it wasn't pork.

He ate quickly, after his habit, and called the Mexican over again to complain about the quality of the meal and to repeat the offer of the gold piece in exchange for useful information. Then he hurried outside without leaving a tip, as much to get away from the smell of the cantina as anything.

Wagon Mound was the grayest, homeliest little town he'd ever seen, and he'd gotten fairly well acquainted with some of the most no-account towns on earth. Here the 'dobe huts were scattered around the flats that ran right up to the face of the foothills. In the heart of the town, a few frame houses were laid out in a more or less regular fashion along a scraped-off piece of desert that passed for a street. Nearby, the usual tumbledown clutter of cantinas, liveries, and smithies stood bleaching in the sun. The town was neither Anglo nor Mexican, but a peculiar mixture of the two built up around a small butte that stood out a way from the foothills themselves—the mound that gave the place its name. What Godforsaken country!

He woke the bay from her doze and led her to the nearest stables, where he bought a bucket of oats and a fresh hay stall for two bits. Then, somewhat reluctantly, he went looking for whatever law there was to be found in Wagon Mound.

There wasn't much, as it turned out.

The constable was a squinty-eyed little Texican well gone in a bottle of cheap rye whiskey. With a little trouble, the big man managed to get out of the Texican that the real law, the deputy sheriff, was off in Las Vegas on business and wasn't expected back for a week. In fact, the deputy only came around to Wagon Mound twice a month, it seemed; if there was trouble, the Texican said, he took care of it himself. Or— and this the big man found more likely—the trouble just played itself out without any interference from the law.

The big man asked the constable if he'd seen a skinny kid, a stranger, around the town. He'd have come from the south or east, out of the flat grass plains, most likely.

The Texican sucked at his bottle a long while before answering.

"You're the onliest stranger I seen in some while. Ain't too skinny, though!" He giggled a little and took another long pull on the bottle.

The big man held his temper. "It's worth cash money."

The little man's eyes danced, but he had to shrug. "Ain't seen no strangers. Sorry."

The big man gave him a calculated look of cool violence, but began to move away, in part to save time and in part to bluff the constable.

"Now, wait a minute," the Texican said, plainly trying to think. "There was something. You say it's worth cash money?"

"Such as?"

"Something. Might be about your stranger. Might not. How much is it worth?"

The big man moved in close to the stinking constable. There was the reek of whiskey and stale sweat about him. "Ten dollars if it's for sure about him. Six bits if I'm interested enough. And I'll kick your arse up that damn mountain if you're just fleecing me."

The constable giggled, but he blinked hard, too, trying to clear his mind. He put the bottle aside. "Well, I ain't sure. Hate to give up on a ten dollar piece, but as a officer of the law, I wouldn't steal your money, neither. So however you slice it, six bits is six bits."

The big man waited, allowing his impatience to show around the edges of his mouth and his square, taut jaw.

The Texican tried to smile in the face of the mounting anger, but his courage failed him. He swallowed hard and spoke, the voice coming out in a whine. "Man I know from up to Springer—that's north a piece—come into town t'other day. Said he'd come upon somethin' queer. Found a dead horse 'long a arroyo out near the Canadian."

"A dead horse ain't worth nothing to me. Not six bits."

"This'n was a mouse-colored ridin' horse, at least what was left. The buzzards had done good on it, my acquaintance said. Anyhow, he allows as how somebody'd been ridin' that horse and had kilt it an' taken off walkin', carryin' his saddle an' such. Bootprints went back to the east for a spell, he said."

The big man refused to smile. "Could have been any fool cowboy hereabouts."

"Could have. Don't think so, though. Man who found it said it didn't look like no cow pony, at least not with any brand he knew, an' he knows most of 'em round here. Anyhow, that horse died an' put its rider afoot. That's all I know."

"You said the rider killed it."

"Shot it, so I'm told. Got played out or throwed the rider an' pissed him off, or somethin'. My acquaintance said the horse was shot betwixt the eyes. Put out of its misery, in any case. Or so I'm told."

"And that's all you know?"

"That's it."

"That's not much."

The Texican grinned again and picked up the bottle. "Six bits ain't much money."

"How far from here did your friend find this horse?"

"Didn't say he was a friend. Just a man I know."

"How far?" The big man's patience was wearing thin.

"Can't say. Out on the flat. Twenty miles, mebbe. East. As the crow flies. You can find out for sure in Springer. Ask for Juan Archuleta. Got a big spread near town. He's my acquaintance. Nice fella for a Mexican."

"Christ awmighty." The big man scuffed the toe of his boot into the dirt. He'd lose a lot of valuable time riding all the way to Springer. "This Archuleta speak good English?"

"Sure. Now how 'bout them six bits?"

The big man dug into his pockets and came up with the coins.

The Texican took the money and tried it with his teeth to be sure it was genuine. "This stranger you're lookin' for. He a friend of yours?"

"An acquaintance," the big man said, mimicking the Texican.

The little man pretended not to hear the insult. "You're the law. Bein' a constable myself, I can tell. There a reward out for your 'acquaintance'?"

The big man ignored the question. "Name's Alvarez. Deputy U.S. Marshal Thomas Alvarez, from Abilene."

The Texican whistled softly, but didn't take his eyes off Alvarez just in case there was some reaction. This new information had clearly impressed him. "U.S. Marshal. Shit. Why's a man named Alvarez worried about his Spanish?" He giggled again, stupidly.

The marshal's face blackened with real anger. "You got your six bits. You got anything else to tell me, we'll talk. You want to pass the time of day, do it with someone else."

The Texican backed up a few feet, beyond the big man's reach. "Now, hold on. I'm a lawman, too. Ain't no call to get rude with me, Marshal."

Alvarez spit into the dust as if he had something profoundly distasteful in his mouth. "You give lawmen a bad name." Almost without conscious thought, he brought his right hand to rest easily on the butt of his revolver.

The constable's Adam's apple bobbed up and down, and he took another drink, this time because he needed it. "Well, you just look up Old Man Archuleta, then. He'll fill you in about that dead horse. Your stranger ridin' a mouse-colored horse?"

"Maybe. Maybe not."

The little man grinned. Another swallow of whiskey fortified his courage. "If he was, you owe me ten dollars," he said.

"Minus the six bits."

"If you say so, Marshal."

Alvarez smiled, but it was the cold, cruel, violent smile that he had become so good at over the years. "I do. I will look up your friend Archuleta and just see about that horse."

*   *   *

Alvarez went hunting for a decent boardinghouse—one without bedbugs, preferably—but his mind wasn't really on where he wanted to spend the night. Mostly, he was weighing the drunk Texican's doubtful honesty. The marshal was good at sizing up people's integrity. He had to be, in his line of work.

It was a lead-pipe cinch that the little weasel constable couldn't be relied upon. No damned doubt of that. Drifters like him could wear a badge in one town and rustle cattle off the range or rob a bank in the next town without ever skipping a beat. Still, it was also a certainty that Shingleton had been riding a dun horse the last time anyone had seen him, probably the one he was known to have stolen from that west Kansas farmer. That would explain no local brand. The only thing that didn't figure was why Shingleton would have taken off hiking back toward the east. What was there in that direction for the kid to be interested in?

He found a boardinghouse that looked decent enough and gave the weak-chinned old spinster who owned the place a dollar for the night's lodging and breakfast. The woman eyed him suspiciously, but she took his money and showed him to a room that wasn't much larger than the swaybacked old bedstead in it. The ticking was worn and filled with knotted horsehair that felt more like rocks than bedding when he sprawled across it. The old woman stayed in the doorway as he tried the bed, and she scowled fiercely at him when he put his booted feet up on the ticking, but he just scowled back, and finally she went away.

The place smelled of too many former occupants and burnt-dry New Mexican dust and coal-oil smoke. He closed his eyes. He had to use the privy out back. The beans and steak stuck like a lump of wet clay in his stomach. And to top everything else, he had to ride the foothills trail tomorrow to try to find some old Mexican bastard so he could talk to him about a dead horse.

"God, I hope old Archuleta speaks good English," Alvarez

said to himself. He'd have to remember not to use his surname. If the old man caught even a hint that the marshal had Spanish blood, he'd be like all the rest of them, spitting out that gibberish as fast as he could.

Alvarez hauled himself out of bed, went to the privy, and managed at last to work the clay lump down a little with a good belch. Back in the tiny room, he took off his boots and pants for the first time in several days and washed up in the porcelain basin the old woman had set out. Then he stretched out crosswise over the mattress so his six-foot-three frame would fit. Within a few minutes, he was sound asleep.

Even in sleep, he kept his right hand on the oiled leather holster and the butt of his old Smith and Wesson .38.

CHAPTER 5

CORA Diemert stood in the shade of the chicken coop and watched the young man work. He was surely a demon for hard labor, even if it was because he wanted to keep his part of their bargain so she'd keep hers. A rick of firewood cut, water hauled, and scrub brush cleared from around the fence—that was what he had to do before she'd let him hitch up her buckboard and run it in to Springer or Wagon Mound, where he could buy a horse.

She was taking a calculated risk, after all, and so she had to try to get as much out of it as possible. If he stole the mule she'd promised to loan him, which was certainly possible, at least she'd have this heavy work done and the brush cleared away so the cowboys couldn't hide there when next they came to visit. On the other hand, he might turn out to be an honest man, and if so . . . well, she'd have to pay the livery man in town something to board the mule for a few days, and she reasoned this Bill Smith might as well help make payment with his toil.

The truth of it was that she couldn't help but admire Smith, or whatever his name was, at least in a grudging way. He was a hard worker, a man not afraid to sweat. And he was quiet, keeping mostly to himself. Her Henry had been just the opposite, a talker and a boastful man, full of himself and his dreams and schemes. When Cora had been young, she had loved that in him, but the Cherokee strip and now this New Mexico wilderness had cured her of that. She saw no percentage to be gained in a man who talked and schemed and was forever restless. Especially when he up and died on top of it. She still loved Henry well enough, she reckoned, but mostly because she had lived with him for all those years and had borne his children and watched one of them die.

Oh, there was no denying that it was the child's death that had really broken him. As, in fact, it had broken her. His dreams had once been insistent dreams, filled with glory and good things: orchards and fine fruit trees and cattle grazing on lush grass and rows of beehives to provide a bounty of clear honey and good wax for fine candles. And then their boy had died. At that moment, in the instant when her own grief had made her powerless to prevent the disaster brewing inside him, his once-noble dreams had crumbled into darkness.

After a suitable time, when the trappings of their grief had fallen away and life once again appeared to be normal, Henry had talked again of herds of sleek cattle in their golden years ahead, but this time the visions were based on a craving for new lands, far away from their home church in the valley and its forbidding graveyard. It was as if Henry had suddenly come to expect only disappointment and disaster in Missouri, and expectation that only a westering move could avoid. So orchards and fine pastures had in time become a quarter section of poor ground and a soddy; and that had given way, too, until there was nothing but a few half-starved cattle and overwhelming debt and no future.

Cora's Grandmother Galt—that great, wise, shriveled woman who had raised her—had always said that time heals all wounds. In that, if in nothing else in her life, she had been wrong; some wounds only festered and worsened with the passing of the years. And that fact, too, added an extra measure of continuing sadness to Cora's life.

Bill Smith leaned on the handle of the hoe and mopped his forehead. "Ma'am, I do b'lieve you'll be havin' some company directly," he said quietly.

She only half heard and paid him no attention; she was still lost in the painful past.

"Mrs. Diemert!" Smith said with more than a touch of

urgency, as if to awaken her. "There's riders coming up from the south!" He was straining already to get a better view of the southern horizon hidden in the mesas and chop hills. He dropped the hoe and edged toward the shed, where his guns and saddlebags still lay among the scattered chicken straw.

She recovered with a start and turned to look, too. She shielded her eyes against the afternoon sun. Yes, there was no mistaking it: a cloud of dust, big enough to be coming from a half-dozen or more well-mounted men. Ignoring Smith, she headed for the house—for the shotgun.

Panic, that old and familiar enemy, clutched at her, and she had to fight it down through sheer willpower. Panic addled the mind and caused the senses to become traitors. Oncoming riders presented a test that had to be met. Without panic.

Cora shooed the children indoors just as she had three days before, when she'd seen the stranger coming in from the southeast; this time, Joe brought her the shotgun, loaded, without being asked.

Lord God in Heaven, she prayed. *Lord God.* . . . But an ending didn't come to her; what she prayed for would best remain unspoken, unthought.

She could make out six of them, trotting in on their bandylegged cow ponies that were weighted down with leather and rope and men. Little men on little horses, riding easily and laughing as they came. She cocked the hammers. She had seen these men before. They were from the Miller place, the biggest of the spreads down near Fort Sumner.

The men came on, and she stood her ground, entirely forgetting about the young man with the hoe as she concentrated on the riders.

They drew up their ponies in front of her, but a little way off, and for a moment or two they mumbled among themselves, as if unsure of what it was they wanted to do.

Well, she'd help them.

"What do you want now?" she called out, her voice husky with anger.

"Just passin' through, missus," one of them, older than the rest, answered almost casually. "We're just checkin' out the land hereabouts for strays from our remuda."

She recognized this one now. He was the foreman. "I have no horses on my place. Least of all from your remuda."

"They'd be the Box E brand, missus. Miller's Box Elder Ranch. You don't mind if we look?"

"I do."

The man shrugged. "We have to find our horses. They've been rustled."

"They're not on my place."

The cowboy stared at the ground for a few seconds—to screw up his courage, she thought—then he nodded, just once. In answer to that unspoken command, all the ponies leaped forward, and before she could bring the great gun up they were swarming around her, the men whooping and stirring up the air and slapping at their horses' flanks with their broad felt hats. Then they were past her, stampeding for the little garden. In two seconds they'd overrun it, cutting her vegetables to ribbons.

Her senses returned. She jerked the gun up and sent a load of buckshot flying after them, but there was no way to tell through the cloud of yellow dust whether she'd hit anything. She fired at them again and snapped the barrels open to reload.

The cowboys came circling back around the house and surrounded her while she was still fighting the paper cartridges. One of the young ones swooped down as he galloped past and snatched the shotgun from her hands. She tried to hang on, but he was stronger; the momentum of horse and rider together made her powerless to resist.

"Any of you boys hit?" the foreman asked as they calmed their mounts and crowded around in front of her. The gang smelled of fear and horse sweat and liquor.

"Old Dandy took some shot in the rump, I think," one said.

"Got me a pellet in the shoulder," said another, and he showed his bloodied arm to prove it.

The foreman looked over the wound quickly and leaned far over his saddle horn toward her, his lips drawn into a thin, tight line over his teeth.

"You could have killed one of my men, missus. Now, you've been warned before. This is Box Elder range. Shootin' at us'll only get you hurt! We don't want to harm you, but you're stealin' our stock and squattin' on our range, neither of which is healthy. You take to blastin' at us with that scattergun, and we'll quit being polite." He looked over his shoulder at the cowboy with the rump-shot horse. "How bad's your mount, Rawley?"

"Hard to tell, Boss. I reckon he'll live." The horse was dancing and twisting, trying to get away from the stinging pain in its rear.

"Well, we can't be so sure. So you'll have to pay us for that horse, missus. Plus the mounts from our remuda, of course. Where are your animals?"

She glared at the foreman and reached for her shotgun, but the kid holding it jerked on the reins, and his horse backed away, keeping it out of her reach.

"I seen a mule back there," the kid said.

The foreman nodded. "That'll do for starters. Rawley, you commandeer that mule in fair trade for a rump-shot horse."

The one called Rawley grinned and turned his mount toward the livestock pens behind the house.

"You got no right to take my stock," she said coldly through her teeth.

"And you got no right to be on this land, missus. You want to stay healthy, you'll get off. Next time, if you're still here, we'll bring torches and burn you out." He grabbed the shotgun from his companion and swung it over his head and threw it as far out into the sand and scrub grass as he could. "You coming, Rawley?"

"Yessir!" Rawley shouted from the little corral alongside the barn. He already had a rope around the neck of one of the mules.

That was when they heard the whine of the carbine. Rawley's hat flew off his head; the concussion of the bullet passing within an inch of his scalp sent him flying out of the saddle and onto the ground. The mule brayed and backed away, and before any of the cowboys had time to react, Bill Smith stepped into the sunlight from the darkness of the chicken coop. He levered a shell into the carbine and pointed it at a spot between the foreman's eyes.

"You get off her place. Now." Smith was deadly calm, his flat Kansas accent adding an extra measure of determination to the words. His finger rested as easily on the trigger as if he were taking a sighting for target practice.

"Who the hell are you?" the foreman asked, but he didn't take his eyes off the small black hole in the end of the rifle.

"Just move," Smith replied.

"You all right, Rawley?"

The downed cowboy picked himself up and scrambled after his hat and caught up the reins of his horse. The bullet had singed his hair and the tumble had dirtied him some, but he wasn't hurt.

Without moving his feet or his gaze from the foreman's face, Smith swung the rifle around and sent another shot so close to Rawley that he hit the dirt again. In one smooth motion, Smith cocked the carbine and picked up his aim on the leader.

"The next one kills his horse. Or him, if I miss a little. Or you, just because I feel like it. Now, you all just leave the mule and get off her place. The way I figure it, a little buckshot in a horse's tail or a cowboy's shoulder is only fair exchange for the turnips you trampled."

The foreman glowered, but he made no threatening moves. "This ain't your concern, mister."

"Leave the mule and git!" Smith jabbed the rifle muzzle at them. "I ain't sayin' it again."

The foreman pulled up on the reins and his horse stepped back a few feet. "Awright. But we'll be back."

"You come back and you'll get more of the same."

The one called Rawley mounted gingerly and joined his companions, leaving the mule standing alone, the short rope still tied around her neck. The foreman looked around at his men, then stabbed the sharp rowels of his spurs into his horse's side. The animal leaped, and with a vicious tug on the reins, the man turned the horse away from the house. The others followed, cantering away, but when they reached the opening in the bobwire, the foreman swung around again.

"This is Box Elder range! You squatters better never forget that!" Then they all put spurs to their cow ponies, and in a few minutes they were out of sight.

Cora Diemert hurried after her shotgun, checked it for damage, and reloaded quickly. Even as she did, her eyes scanned over the brushland and the mesas; she half expected the cowboys to make good on their threat immediately. By the time she had assured herself that they were truly gone, Bill Smith had vanished, too, back into the deep shadows of the shed.

They ate a late supper in silence at her little table, and the children, taking their cue from the grownups, were unusually quiet. Cora had picked some fresh greens she's salvaged and had wilted them with hot lard and a dash of vinegar. There was cold corn bread and molasses laid out alongside.

"I'd of been pleased to fix a chicken for you, Mr. Smith. For what you did for us," she said softly.

"You'll need the birds for the eggs." He didn't look at her, but only sopped up the molasses with a piece of crumbly corn bread.

"I surely will, but fresh meat is good, too, now and again. Especially when there's something to celebrate. Chicken from time to time is a real luxury out here. We used to have pork regular, and even some beef once in a great while, when Henry got around to doing some butchering . . ." Her voice trailed off.

"They'll come back for sure, you know," he said.

To hide the quick flame of embarrassment, she tucked her head as if she were busy with her own food. "In Missouri, we used to get the whole family together for butchering. The women would scrape casings and make sausages while the men did the killing and gutting and singeing and cutting of the hams. My mother used to make head cheese and scrapple that was the talk of the county."

"You know they'll be back," he repeated, so softly that his voice had a gentleness about it that it had not had before.

Her hand trembled, and she put down her fork.

"They've come before, so yes, they will come again." The flinty ferocity in her tone did not hide the underlying fear. "They're trying to frighten us off our own place, Mr. Smith, but they won't do it."

"I shamed 'em today, Mrs. Diemert. Made it personal. I'm sorry for that, because it'll only bring 'em on faster. To settle a score with me as well as with you."

"Don't worry about that. I'm beholden to you as it is. Wasn't for you, they'd have taken the mule, and maybe worse."

He smiled weakly and pushed his wilted greens around on his plate. "To be absolutely honest, I should of let 'em take her. Then they'd of thought they were big brave men and maybe they'd of left you alone for a while. Once I shamed 'em, I just guaranteed they'd be back to get even."

"I don't know. . . ."

They finished eating, and she sent the children outside to

play in the pool of yellow light that spilled out of the opened
doorway, but with a warning to Joe to keep an ear to the
dusk-darkened open country for any sound that might mean
the return of the cowboys. While the children were outside,
Cora cleared the dishes and washed them in the bit of warm
water she'd kept heated on the back of the stove, alongside
the coffee pot.

"Why *did* you help me, Mr. Smith?" She did not look at
him.

"Shouldn't have, I reckon."

"But you did. Why?"

He cleared his throat and sniffed before answering. Once
again, the words came out soft and slow and gentle. "Guess I
don't like seein' no man take advantage of a woman. 'Spe-
cially one that did me a good turn of takin' me in when I was
in need." He started to say something else, but changed his
mind.

"And that's all?"

He remained silent.

"When will you be leaving us, then?"

"Soon as I earn the right to borrow a mule for a day."

"You did that this afternoon."

He smiled thinly. "Then soon, I suppose."

He dried the dishes for her while she parched and ground
the next day's coffee and put out clean china cups for the
two of them. Her hands trembled so that the china rattled
when she put the cups on the saucers; in the next instant,
she felt her knees starting to go beneath her. Only sheer
force of will kept them from buckling. Recently she was
finding it harder than ever to find that reserve of strength
within herself.

"Mr. Smith?"

"Yes'm?"

"I'd be obliged . . . I mean we'd all be so beholden to you
if you'd stay with us a few more days. In case those cowboys
come back again or something."

"I need to be goin'."

She turned to face him full on, not minding suddenly that she was flushed from the mingling of shame and pride that had made her ask such a thing of this man. A stranger who had come unbidden and unwanted to her and who had so completely aroused first her fears and then her feelings of gratitude and a hunger for companionship.

"I'd . . . truly be beholden," she said, and this time her voice was tiny and afraid.

He blinked once and looked away from her, moved by her pain as much as by his own confession. "Miz Diemert, I need to be goin' on. Truly."

"Why? I need you here."

The boldness and simplicity of her admission startled them both—her for having said it, and him for having been so unprepared to hear it. He waited while she poured the coffee before he made any attempt to answer.

"I need to put some miles between me and this place," he said at length as he cradled the hot coffee cup in his hands. He knew he could have remained quiet and she would not have asked him again. He put the cup down, stirred the scalding coffee with a spoon, and poured some of it into the chipped saucer to cool.

"You're running from the law," she said.

He brought his eyes up to hers for part of a heartbeat and then looked back at the saucer and the steam rising from the coffee.

"Well, we'd be beholden if you'd stay awhile anyway," she said, having gotten all the confirmation she needed.

"It ain't big trouble, Miz Diemert. Honest."

Now it was her turn to keep quiet.

"Look, you been good to me, ma'am. I appreciate that. Reckon I could of stayed here a couple of more days, too, but them fellas is apt to tell somebody I was here."

"Then it was big trouble."

"No, ma'am. Not really. But the law. . . . It's just them cowboys is apt to spill the beans on me."

"They don't care about you. They just want this place. For Miller, their boss. It's just the land."

"After today, they care."

The argument hardened her a little, and she set her jaw. "Then you must do as your conscience commands, Mr. Smith," she said.

"Then I'll go." He drank the cooled coffee from the saucer and wiped his mouth on his sleeve. Because he knew the next thing could not be avoided, he couldn't help grinning just a little in spite of himself. "Leastwise, I'll go as soon as I reckon I've earned the use of the mule. Guess that will take me a few more days of chopping wood." He lifted the coffee cup to his lips and blew softly across it, scattering the steam.

CHAPTER 6

TOM Alvarez rode into the open country south of Old Man Archuleta's place with a renewed thirst for the chase. Lawing was often hard, bone-grinding work, and almost always it was a mixture of boredom and disappointment that made the occasional dangerous moments something to be looked forward to. In tracking work like this, good leads were few and far between, and when you got one, it usually petered out to nothing after a while. But every now and then, a stroke of luck or some dazzling insight cut through the tedium and made being a marshal worth all the effort. In a real sense, it was still the thrill of the hunt that drew Alvarez to his job and kept him at it.

Running into that drunken constable sure wasn't a piece of insight, but it *was* just the kind of luck he needed to best Ben Comstock or any of the others who might be out chasing Billy Shingleton. One dead horse out in the middle of nowhere wouldn't raise an eyebrow beyond Wagon Mound; so Ben Comstock or Arnold Toothacker or Black Jack Griswold from over in Santa Fe or any of the other federal officers on the lookout for Shingleton would never know that the kid had managed to get himself put afoot out here in these Godforsaken chop lands on the edge of the Staked Plains.

Llano Estacado, he said to himself as he spurred his big horse into a hard center. It sounded better in Spanish, he had to admit, and he laughed out loud. Just now, his lifelong struggle with—or against—his father's native tongue seemed of no importance at all. Hell, he'd even been able to get by with Archuleta, whose English was really abysmal. He laughed again.

That old man was a corker, all right. A cross between a big-time braggart rancher like those Alvarez had met in the heart of the *llano* in Texas and the dour, tight-lipped sod-busters who dotted that endless stretch of prairie west of Abilene. Like the ranchers, Archuleta was a strutter, a careful dresser who smoked good cigars and talked big; like the sod-busters, he was shrewd and calculating behind the eyes, always weighing his words before he said them, even the big talk, always saying just a little less than enough. Archuleta would be one hell of a poker player, the kind who would never once tip his hand. And all of it was wrapped up in a brown wrinkled package of a man not five-feet-two. Of course, most of these things Alvarez had learned before he ever rode out to the man's place, because he had made careful inquiries of the old-timers around Wagon Mound and Springer. But Archuleta had been everything and more than the boys had said he was.

He'd been born of dirt-poor *peon* parents, but somewhere along the way, by virtue of intellect and hard work, he'd proven himself useful to some Democrat ranchers, including one named Miller who ran the biggest spread between Santa Fe and the Texas border. With the ranchers' help, Archuleta had managed to get a few head of breeder cattle to start a herd. Almost every cow had a different brand—the story went—but no one bothered to complain, not with Archuleta's friends behind him. More importantly, the old man had finagled a way to get the territorial legislature to assign him title to one of the old-time Spanish land grants. Even though it gave him no real ownership of so much as an acre of ground, it had made him very tall in the eyes of the other Mexicans around the area. He was in every way a feudal duke without a duchy. Between Miller's beeves and the strong backs of the willing *peons,* Archuleta had become a powerful man.

Alvarez had never liked such men, who used others to get ahead. But Archuleta was an original, and Alvarez found himself with a grudging admiration for the man. Of course, there was no doubt now that the carcass of the dun-colored horse Archuleta had stumbled upon while returning from a visit to relatives in Santa Rosa was Billy Shingleton's. The old man was enough of a cowman to have checked the brand on the dead horse and marked it down in his little brand book. A circle with a line through it, he had said. The Broken O from the small herd belonging to Oliver Orman, the Kansas farmer who'd lost a dun riding horse to Billy Shingleton. That Broken O brand had been seen several times in the Panhandle country, the last place that Alvarez had been dead certain he was on the right trail. Now it had been seen on a carcass west of the headwaters of the Canadian.

The important thing was—where had the rider gone after his horse went down?

No telling, Archuleta had said, his little black eyes shining in the sunlight of the veranda. Outside of Springer or Wagon Mound, this was a lonely country. In town, a man afoot carrying a saddle would stick out like a sore thumb. Maybe he's stolen another horse, Alvarez had offered. The old man had only smiled. Maybe he was *muerte,* Archuleta had said. Dead. In that big country, it was always easier for someone to hide the bones of a man than the bones of a horse.

Muerte. And Archuleta had grinned when he said it.

No, Alvarez reckoned that Billy Shingleton was not dead. Dead men didn't walk off into the desert with a saddle and the all-important saddlebags; and from the way Archuleta had described the horse, it didn't seem that Shingleton had been jumped by anyone. The horse had just given out, probably, and why not? The kid had never been easy on horses. None of his family were. So the horse went down and Shingleton had taken off on foot. But where? It *was* damn lonely country, and no kid afoot had shown up at either of the two nearby towns. Everyone vouched for that. And from where Archuleta said he'd found the horse, it would have been too far to hike south to Santa Rosa. Hell, Shingleton would have been damn near twenty-five miles from Springer! A solid twenty even if he walked it straight and true, which was a sizeable order for a kid carrying a saddle through rough country he'd never seen before.

Which, of course, was also Tom Alvarez's big problem, and he knew it. Like Shingleton, he was a newcomer. Even with a decent map, he had to go by dead reckoning as often as not. There was a dismal sameness to the rolling vista of saltbush and grama grass. The bench buttes and mesas all looked alike, and when you figured one of them was a mile or so away, it turned out to be three or four. The little dry washes coming down from them never really went anywhere, or at least they never connected to a proper river that he could locate on the map. Or maybe it was just that here, where it was so dry, even the Canadian and the Cimarron weren't much more than washes with a little damp gravel in them.

In the flat emptiness of Kansas, where Alvarez was used to hunting, the streams were like the rungs on a ladder. You knew where you were in that country, with the counties and towns and even God's own rivers laid out in a geometric certainty, and the settlers everywhere in their soddies and dugouts busily bringing the soil to the plow. Here, on uninhabited open range that hadn't yet been surveyed for homesteaders and might never be, he could only guess at where he was.

Alvarez stopped his horse atop a low mesa six or seven miles south of Archuleta's big adobe hacienda. Except for the mountains on the western edge of the horizon, the country was the same in all directions—broken gray-green plains stubbled with mesas and scrub brush and an occasional broad, low mesquite; and there was no living animal for all the eye could see, except the scattering of black birds, the vultures riding the winds a thousand feet above the surface.

His mare snuffled and shifted uneasily beneath him.

There was a storm brewing, and the horse felt it. Off to

the west, the first pine-studded ramparts of the Sangre de Cristos were already being swallowed up in the heavy blue-black of the rain clouds that had been building all day, thrusting their anvil-shaped tops far into the sky.

He smoked a cigaret more from habit than desire, consulted his useless map again, and nudged his horse in the general direction that Archuleta had indicated. First, he would find the horse's bones to see if that gave him a clue. Just in case, he loaded his short Winchester carbine so he'd have a little more range than he'd get from the Smith and Wesson.

To his great surprise, he found the skeleton easily. It was sprawled out in a little low spot just as Archuleta had described it. By his figuring, this place was less than five miles from the main road into Wagon Mound, so he'd been hot on Shingleton's trail all along—had, in fact, probably passed him. That was some comfort.

The dun horse's bones were picked clean and already bleaching in the sun. Judging from the leavings, the coyotes and tawny southern wolves had done some fighting over this carcass. Bits and pieces of the leg bones were strewn about, and the ribs lay cracked open and gnawed. He picked up some of the pieces, looking to discover what might have brought the horse down, but in the end all he had to go by was the skull. He couldn't tell what had caused the horse to falter, but he was sure Billy had put the dun out of its misery. The spent slug still rattled in the braincase.

Alvarez laughed again. Kill the horse and get left afoot! Well, Billy boy, it's what you deserve!

Alvarez left the carcass and rode on, crisscrossing the arroyos and skirting the patches of short grass. He was too intent on looking for signs now to be bothered by the growing heaviness in the air. He rode east all the way to a brackish little stream that he guessed was probably the root stream of the South Canadian, then he rode back again across the mesas. Wagon ruts showed up here and there, and he stopped to inspect a couple of deserted line shacks the ranchers used during roundup, but there were no signs of recent human habitation. Somewhere, nestled in the gullies or between the mesas, he knew there were one or two squatters' huts, because that was what Archuleta had told him, but they sure weren't easy to find. All he had to go on for now were wagon tracks that went nowhere and line shacks that housed nothing but pack rats and black widow spiders. Not much. This was, indeed, Godforsaken country.

After several hours, the black thunderheads moving relentlessly across the sky swallowed up the sun. Alvarez spurred his mount to the top of one broad mesa several miles east of where he'd found the horse. It seemed almost pointless to him, but before the light was gone entirely, he wanted one more chance to take a look around from a high place. While his horse cropped at the grass, he climbed a jumble of broken slab rock and scanned the horizon. To the west, toward Wagon Mound, and to the northwest in the direction of Springer, there was nothing. He turned south and east. Again, nothing. No life at all. Not even the lazy drifting of the vultures. They were gone to their hidden nests to wait out the storm—which was what he should do, Alvarez knew, and as quickly as possible. He knew he should get in the lee of one of the big buttes and hunker down and wait it out. Night was coming on and wild weather with it, and in all the broad expanse of country that gave way to the rolling plains toward Texas, there was nothing.

Or, perhaps, there was something after all. A streak of cloud, maybe. Or a trick of the eye.

Or smoke, a thin blue wisp of it rising straight into the still, heavy air of late afternoon. Two or three miles away. Maybe more. Distances played tricks on the eye out here: it could be five miles. He went back to the horse and dug out his binoculars.

There was a moment when he thought he'd lost the wisp,

but then he found it again, brought closer and sharper by the glasses. Yes, it was smoke. But how far? He couldn't tell, even now, and the undulations in the broken plains hid whatever was causing the smoke. He took his bearings as well as he could and mounted up. He'd go have a look-see if the storm held off long enough.

The air itself was a crushing burden to both man and horse as they rode. His shirt stuck to his back, and sweat trickled out from under his hatband and down into his eyes. The big horse plodded along listlessly, as if it carried two riders on its back.

The sun was swallowed up entirely in the massing clouds, and the whole sky took on a gray, shimmering quality that made it hard to distinguish where open sky ended and the thin, hazy vanguard of the cloud began. The man could no longer see the smoke; and without the sun, he wasn't positive that he was moving in a straight line toward it. Dead reckoning was all he had now, and under the circumstances, it was very little.

He stopped several times and turned in the saddle to look west, into the heart of the storm, to watch the lightning playing through the thick banks of cloud. The thunder was still only a vague rumble. It reminded him, surprisingly, of the sound of the Union mortars muffled by the miles of dense Missouri timber—the first and only sounds of the war that had reached his parents' homestead back in those dark days. Funny, he thought, that lightning and thunder in New Mexico should remind him suddenly of a war a quarter century gone.

He pressed on, trying his best as he went to keep the horse going in that straight line of dead reckoning.

He found the smoke, and the storm found him simultaneously.

At first it was only a light rain, with big cold drops that splashed the size of silver dollars on his dusty clothes. In that sprinkling rain he saw the blue smoke of a wood fire, much nearer now, apparently just over the rise ahead. Even a blind man could find it from here, he thought. Even in a blinding rain.

He did not have to wait. Within a heartbeat, the slashing wind and driving, piercing sting of hard rain stole the smoke away and engulfed his world, near and far alike, in pounding grayness. There was hail, too; little grapeshot hail stung his cheek and the exposed back of his neck and flattened the crown of his high black hat. The horse stopped cold and swung its rump into the rain and put its head down almost between its front knees.

"Damn!" he said aloud, but the wind snatched the sound away. He swore again and prodded the horse with his spurs; but the spurring did no good, and the curses, like the first, were lost to the wind and hail and the sharper crackle of close thunder grown suddenly too close. Though he was wet through already, he managed to pull a slicker out of the tight roll of bedding tied behind the cantle and get it draped around his shoulders. The drumming of rain and hail on the oilcloth was so loud that he couldn't even hear himself now.

The damnings were pointless, anyhow. He'd been in enough of these summer thunderstorms to know that there was nothing to be done but wait out the worst of it. After all, the heart of these desert thunderstorms was usually small, and this one would be sweeping eastward on the wind after a few minutes, likely; surely it would be gone before full nightfall.

The hard violence of the storm didn't last, as he had figured. Within a quarter hour, the hail stopped altogether and the downpour abated with the wind, but the rain contin-ued as a steady, cold drizzle that told him he wasn't so lucky after all. The air temperature had fallen ten or fifteen degrees. The gray wall of the cloudburst had moved on, but looking west he could see no reemergence of the sun in its wake. All the way to the invisible mountains the sky was low and dark and leaden and full of rain. In fact, the rain made the sky seem to meet the earth and swallow it up.

He got the horse moving again, and at the top of the rise, he saw the ranch. A half mile away, nestled between this rise and a low mesa, lay a tiny adobe house and a jumble of outbuildings and small corrals scattered around a windmill and water tank and a huge lone cottonwood tree. Full darkness was coming on fast; he could make out a faint light in one window of the house, but beyond that, the place showed no sign of life. No huddled horses, no brace or two of mules in the corrals, no rain-drenched dogs shivering in the doorway. Nothing. But maybe he just couldn't see.

Alvarez started to spur the horse gently in the ribs to move her down off the rise, but he held back at the last moment, reining in to hold her on the slope.

Something in the back of his mind, that sixth sense that he depended on for life itself, counseled caution, just as something also told him he'd found his quarry at last. He had been on Billy Shingleton's trail for a long time, and his marshal's instincts were sure: this place would be where he would find the kid. Still, there was hesitancy in his bones.

Even if the kid was in that house, Alvarez knew he could approach without much fear of being seen because of the rain and darkness. But once he got there, once he got beyond whatever fence or gate the rancher might have, and he stood in the yard all cold and waterlogged, he'd be an easy target for a sharpshooting youngster holed up inside. And there was always the chance that the kid was hiding out back, beyond the house, in one of the outbuildings.

Alvarez considered and then dismissed the possibility. If Billy was here—and he was, Alvarez knew it—he'd be inside the house, keeping warm and dry. Which meant that he couldn't escape, even though he damn well could make life uncomfortable—if not uncomfortably short—for the marshal.

Alvarez swore again at his luck and sat back in the saddle for a spell, waiting and watching.

The rain grew steadily colder as he waited. The false twilight had long since merged into the blackness of night. Still, Alvarez kept his watch, focusing on the little spot of soft yellow light that shimmered and swam and sometimes nearly disappeared in the waves of rain that fell in the intervening distance. After a time, all conscious thought, all sense of alertness drifted from him; he was only a pair of eyes peering through the rain at a warm yellow spot of light. The horse, as if understanding, grew restless and took to walking slowly back and forth along the top of the slope to keep warm, never going so far that Alvarez had to take his eyes off the house.

A vague sense of familiarity rose within the marshal, yet it remained far enough beyond his consciousness that he need not express it in words. Family, that's what this place evoked. The old home place. His youth, and other rainstorms. And other times of danger, too. Mostly family, and Ma and peaceful nights . . .

When the door opened, spilling another pool of yellow light into the yard, Alvarez jumped as if he'd been shot. In one heartbeat, all his faculties snapped alert. He jerked the reins hard to turn the horse so he would be directly facing the house and his right hand found the butt of the Smith and Wesson beneath the slicker.

He peered hard through the rain to see if he could make out a human shape at the door. There was one all right, but the distance was so great and the rain so heavy that he couldn't tell whether it was a man or a woman. Then a shadow moved in front of the light, cutting it off. The door had closed.

Alvarez remained rigid, scarcely breathing. Had someone gone outside to use the privy? Hardly likely. Any sane person would use a slop jar on a night like this. Unless maybe Shingleton already was sensing the marshal's presence? But that wasn't likely, either. Perhaps it was someone who just wanted to look out into the rain and the nighttime, to see how hard it was really coming down.

His hunch told him no, and Alvarez trusted his hunches. Someone had, in fact, gone outside in spite of the rain. So he waited. And this time the plan that had been formulating in the back of his mind began to fall into place. So, when the door opened again a few minutes later and the shadow moved across it, he was ready. He loosened the Smith and Wesson in its holster and threw back the slicker and withdrew his short carbine from the boot. He loaded the rifle and nudged his horse down the grade toward the house.

The mare slipped in the sand and wet grass and the darkness, but she was a sure-footed beast for her size, and she kept going.

Alvarez stopped inside the barbed wire gate, not thirty yards short of the house.

"Hallo the house!" he shouted, making sure that he was loud enough to be heard above the rain.

Nothing.

"Hallo the house!"

A shadow passed between the light and the window. Someone was watching.

"I'm United States Marshal Thomas Alvarez, hunting a fugitive. I have a warrant!"

Before he could repeat it, the door opened, and he could make out a woman's figure silhouetted against the lamplight. She said something to someone inside, and a few seconds later a child appeared in the doorway with the lighted lantern. The woman did not reach for the lantern; instead, Alvarez could see that she was cradling a weapon in her arms.

"Come close, you!" the woman called out to him above the rain's sizzle.

Alvarez cocked his Winchester and nudged the big horse forward toward the light. He planned to stop just short of the spot where she would be able to see him well enough to draw a bead, but as he drew closer it was plain that she wouldn't have to be much of a marksman: she hefted a shotgun in a most businesslike manner. He pulled up on the reins and and the horse stepped back a few feet into deeper shadow.

"Come closer, mister, so I can see you."

"Pardon, ma'am, but I believe in being careful. You with that scattergun and all."

"What do you want?"

"Told you, ma'am. I'm a United States Marshal. Name's Thomas Alvarez, from Abilene, Kansas. I'm searching for a fugitive wanted for murder and bank robbery."

"Ain't any murderer here, mister."

"Didn't say there was, ma'am. Mind if I come in out of the wet?"

"I mind."

"It's mighty cold out here."

"I don't have any place for strangers. It's your own fault if you got caught out on a night like this. So say your piece and go."

"I have been, ma'am," he said as gently and reasonably as he could, though he didn't let go his grip on the Winchester. "I'm looking for a fugitive from justice. A young man name of Bill Shingleton, though he may be using another name. He and a party of highwaymen robbed a bank in Larned, up in central Kansas, several months back. They killed a bank teller and a town constable to do it, too. The gang split up, but this Shingleton got away with five thousand dollars in cash. We got the rest of them. Arrested two and killed one in a gunfight near Salina. I figure by now the ones we arrested are waiting to hang if they haven't swung already. This Bill Shingleton—he's the youngest of three brothers involved— he was traced into this part of New Mexico. Seems to have lost his horse and got put afoot nearby your place."

The woman waited a long time before she said anything.

"So now you're going door-to-door in a storm? That's thin, mister."

"This weather come on me and I saw your light. I'd be truly obliged if you could put me up for a while. At least let me rub down my horse and give him a handful or two of oats.

She appeared to be thinking on it for a moment, but her response was exactly what he'd expected.

"No. You go the way you come."

"Not very neighborly, ma'am."

"I'm not your neighbor, Marshal."

"Well, have you seen this Bill Shingleton, then?"

"No one by that name's been by."

"But you've seen a stranger hereabouts?"

"One came by six, seven days back. Got some water at my tank and rode on. Said he was headed for Santa Fe. That's the last stranger I've seen until you."

"Then I'm obliged for the information, ma'am. By the way, you alone?"

She raised the muzzle of the shotgun and pointed it in his direction.

"You git, mister. Rain or no rain, get off my place."

"Suit yourself," he said. "But I'd keep an eye out, were I you. Shingleton's still around here somewhere. I'm sure of it. And don't forget—he's a killer." Alvarez touched the brim of his black hat and wheeled the horse around and rode away. As soon as he was well beyond her sight, he reined in and turned in the saddle to watch the window again. There were shadows moving in there. Two shadows this time. Two adults. His hunch was right. Had to be.

"So," he said to himself, "I'll just sit tight and watch you folks for a while longer, then." He spurred the horse back to the top of the ridge, where he could wait unseen.

The rain, driven on by a wind that had a sharp, cold edge to it, did not let up.

Alvarez broke out his binoculars to help keep watch, but

they were little help. First they fogged over, then rainwater splashed across the front lenses; finally, just when he'd managed to get them cleared the rain picked up, shielding the house from view.

There was nothing to be done but put away the glasses, hunker down, and wait.

An hour passed, then two. This was no usual summer thunderstorm. The water soaked into the gravel along the ridge until the poor soil would hold no more, then it ran down in little rivulets that cut away at the sand and widened into streams that joined together with other streams and swept on to the arroyos that eventually fed into the South Canadian. All the little dry-wash creeks would be flooded come morning.

The big mare began to shudder beneath Alvarez; she, like he, was growing tired and cold. The rain had long since soaked through Alvarez's hat and found its way inside the slicker, drenching his shirt and jacket. He caught himself nodding, and at last he nudged the horse into motion just so the movement might keep them both a little warmer and more alert. It was as bad as any night he could remember.

He tried to survey the house again, but the view was no better than it had been before. For all he could tell, they'd all long since gone to bed.

"Damn! Only a blame fool would sit out in this!" The smart thing to do was to look for a little cover, even if it meant sneaking back into that yard to see if he could get himself and the horse on the dry side of one of the outbuildings without being seen or heard from the house. Maybe come morning, or whenever the weather finally cleared, he could jump Shingleton with ease.

Alvarez prodded the horse once more, and together they started down the slope. It was hard going in the darkness, with the drumming of the rain all around, and the horse balked more at every step. The man dug his knees into the animal's shoulders. They stumbled blindly on toward the house.

Just when Alvarez had allowed himself to relax a little because the horse seemed to be moving on its own, the mare's back feet caught on a tussock of grass and tore it out of the soggy sand. As her back end started to slide in the wet gravel, the horse twisted to right herself, but the slope only shifted out from under her. Her front feet started to splay out, and with one convulsion, she lost her balance completely. Her rump slid down beneath the spread-eagled front feet and she flopped over onto her back and rolled down toward the flat plain below.

Alvarez felt her going and tried to jump clear, but the long slicker caught on the high Spanish-style saddle horn; he managed to get his feet free of the stirrups, but when the horse rolled, he rolled with her. The whole weight of the animal came down on him; he heard and felt the crunching twist as the struggling horse on top of him drove his right leg deep into the sand. Then she was smothering him, lying right on his chest and head. His mouth and eyes filled with hair and water and mud; his ears filled with the panicky screaming of the horse; his brain filled with the white-hot pain in his leg as it twisted again, twisted farther than bone and ligament could stand.

And then he was free of the weight, free of the suffocating horsehide. He tried to sit up, but the stabbing pain in his leg took his breath and strength away, and he fell back into the sand.

Little trickles of water built up on the upslope side of his body as if he were a dam, then broke free and rushed around him. The sand shifted under his hips and back, and he had a vague floating feeling, as if his body were already in the broad river, being pushed through the shallows to a place where his buoyancy would be greater and he might be caught in the current and borne toward the rapids.

The crushing rapids. Death. And release.

He summoned all his strength and shook his head to fight against the fatigue and the pain that would only cloud his senses further.

"I'm losing," he said out loud, as if it meant something. "I'm losing."

Then he spoke again, but it was only incoherent sounds, snatched away once more by the wind and rain.

He fought to bring his mind back, to try to assess the situation coolly and calmly, as Tom Alvarez always had. Always should.

He tried to think through the pain, to locate and analyze it, so that he might know how badly hurt he was. Leg broken. That much he was sure of. But what else? Couldn't say. What was it?

He was passing out.

Suddenly, amazingly, there was a little break in the rain. He came to again, not knowing if it had been seconds or hours since his last clear thought. But this time he was brought back by something other than his own willpower. He felt no driving rain on his face, though he could still hear it all around him, and it was strange and wonderful, this relief from the pelting, stinging icy water. Like the wonderful silence when a great noise subsides.

Alvarez opened his eyes and looked up into the darkness. There was a form bending over him. Someone was sheltering him from the rain.

His heart quickened and he tried to smile.

And then he saw the end of the blue barrel and the twin evil black holes of the shotgun less than a foot from his face.

CHAPTER 7

CORA backed away from the door and eased herself into her chair. She looked for a long time at the man lying in the corner under the pile of blankets she'd put near the stove so he might keep warm. The blankets were steaming, and the man was already asleep, though just a few minutes before he'd been mumbling and groaning and mumbling again from pain and sickness as they had worked on the leg.

Her children peered out from behind the blanket that darkened their bed corner, but after a time they, too, went to sleep. As always, she reached for her Bible before going to bed, and as she did so, her fingers brushed the shotgun still propped up beside her little table.

So now this new complication had come to her, this new trespasser who would—she knew deep down in her bones—change her life. As, indeed, he had already, from the first moment he'd ridden into the yard and ridden out again, leaving behind all those questions about a killing that demanded answering . . .

Bill Smith had come out slowly from his hiding place among the children. Satisfied that the door was closed, he went at once to the window, but Cora intercepted him.

"Stay away. Until he's gone."

"I'm ready," Bill said, and he patted the pistol thrust into his belt.

"Well, I'm not!" She faced him squarely as she snapped out the words, making sure in doing so that she blocked his view outside. "Besides, you don't want him to see you."

"Aw, it's raining too hard."

"He'll see shapes." She pointed at the lantern on the table between them and the window. "He knows you're here. You don't want him to see you first, do you, Mr. Shingleton?"

He flushed red at that, the anger blazing up suddenly in his eyes and working at the corners of his mouth. He made a fist as if to strike out at her, but his anger passed as suddenly as it had come, without a word or deed from him.

"You are Shingleton, the one he's after?"

"I couldn't hear him," he said quietly. "He called me that? Shingleton?"

"He did. Said he was looking for a fugitive. A murderer." And to emphasize her point, she hefted the shotgun.

"Cora, I told you my name is Bill Smith."

She narrowed her eyes to cold slits against the lying.

"Honest. My name is Bill Smith."

"The name's not important. Any fool should have known from the first that you'd lied about the name. It's the other." And she kept the shotgun up, at the ready.

"What other?"

"Why are you hiding from him? You hid from the cowboys the time they came by my place, too. At least you did for a while. So what are you hiding from?" She took a deep breath while she waited for the answer that didn't come. "Was it really murder?"

The blood came back to his face, in shame this time, and it told her everything she had not wanted to know. Even by the fluttering lamplight she could see the hard edge of the lie melt away. And he saw the resolve and fierce strength she had called up from somewhere deep within herself.

He started to protest his innocence again, but instead he gave in with a sigh. He had grown weary suddenly; he found one of her straight-backed old chairs and slumped into it, his feet wrapped uncomfortably around the wooden legs.

"Children, it's time for bed," she said quietly, and once they had disappeared beneath the covers, she put the shotgun down.

They sat quietly until the children were asleep.

"I knew those men were hurt bad," he said softly, almost as if he were talking to himself. "But I didn't know they were dead, Cora. As God is my judge. And as far as that goes, I don't necessarily take the law's word as gospel that they are, neither."

But the story was ready to spill out of him in a torrent in spite of the protest, the way a small crack in a dam gushes water that washes out an ever-larger hole until the reservoir is empty. It was as if he needed to tell her now, as if keeping the truth bottled up for so long had caused it to fester into a boil that needed to bleed freely once it had been lanced. She listened without interrupting him, her rough hands clasped tightly together in her lap, the big knuckles white from squeezing.

The more he talked, the more the unburdening gave him strength and courage to keep going, to tell it all. She gave him not one word of approval, for how could a woman like Cora Diemert approve of robbery and perhaps murder? But she refused to judge him, too. For now, she would weigh the evidence, all of it. The hard work he'd done for her, the driving off of the cowboys, all these things had to be considered, as well as what he had done up in Kansas. She was a fair woman; her people had raised her to be both fair and honest, and when the judgment finally came, it would be only after full consideration of the goodness as well as the evil in him.

After a while, he decided to go back to the beginning, and she let him go.

She reminded him of his own ma, he said, though she was younger by a score of years. But she'd wear out just as his ma had, trying to hold a family together against the hard times and bad troubles like cowboys or drouth or beef at a penny a pound. Then, when it was all said and done, she'd be used up, gone, and the family would split up in spite of her trying, and that would be that.

He fiddled with his fingers for a while as if lost in thought. Then he wondered out loud whether the marshal was telling the truth—that one of the gang was dead. If so, one of his own brothers might be gone. It was hard to think on, but even so . . .

If it was true, it would probably be George, he told her. George never could keep his head down in a fight. Even when they were kids, it had been clear to anyone who paid attention that George was the most reckless of the Shingleton boys, the eldest brother who always had to get himself mixed up in the fistfights and arguments of the others. And it was usually George who wound up getting his nose bloodied or his tooth broken in someone else's fight. Danny, the middle boy—two years younger than George and two years older than Billy—was different. Danny wasn't a coward exactly, but he was decidedly cautious. He was the horse-trader in the clan, the one who would strike the deal that would keep them all out of the trouble George was itching to get them into.

If one of them was dead, it would have to be George. Of course, it might have been that other kid, the one who had helped them with the plan, but he'd been a head-downer like Danny. And if one of the gang had sold Billy out, had told the law where he was heading . . . well, only Danny would have done that. To save his own skin.

Their scheme had seemed so perfect in the beginning. They'd been planning on the Larned job for so long, almost from the days of their first bungling robbery when they'd cleaned out the old German apothecary over in Garden City, west of Dodge. There had been larcenies before that, but the druggist was the first one they'd robbed for money, not just for spite.

Of course, thinking on it now, he had to admit that spite had been a big part of their decision to go after the Larned bank.

Their father had lost a parcel of land to the New England

yankees who owned that bank, and it had been that loss that had driven their family out of Larned to the newer, unclaimed lands to the south and west, closer to the Indian Territory. Billy hadn't even been born when the yankees had robbed his father, but he'd heard all about it. That had been the days of Bleeding Kansas, and the yankees who had controlled the state had been merciless with the poor southern folk like the Shingletons, who'd come up from the Mississippi Delta in the fifties looking for better land and a chance to get shed of plantation aristocrats. In the end, the southerners had done nothing more than trade aristocrats for slick-talking bankers.

Old Man Shingleton had taken the cheating and had gone off to lick his wounds, but as the boys grew up, he never tired of telling them about the bank in Larned and the fat, bulb-nosed yankee who ran it—and of the big black safe where that yankee kept his cash and the deeds to all the land he'd stolen from honest folks. With each retelling, the story had gotten more detailed, more sharply focused, and more hateful. Billy could remember sitting in Sunday school and thinking to himself that Satan must look exactly like a fat banker with a red nose and the blood of honest men beneath his fingernails.

So it had been only natural that once they'd discovered how easy stealing could be that they'd set their sights on the Larned Savings Bank.

And how easy stealing had become!

They had grown up tough kids, dirt-poor and angry, but they weren't the only sons of southern sharecroppers who could say that. How and why they had drifted into petty stealing and lawlessness had seemed almost unimportant once they'd gotten the hang of it and had gotten a goal—Larned. And it had given them a reason for believing in their own code of honor: thieves or cutthroats waylaid and robbed individuals, but bank robbers could be honest men out to right old wrongs.

So they robbed other banks, while they laid their plans for Larned. Ellinwood, coming a few months after the Garden City druggist, had been practice. There were others with them by then, toughs they'd chummed with for years; but the brothers made sure they remained the heart and soul of the gang. The others might come or go as they pleased, in on one robbery, out of another; only the brothers had remained together, ever constant. What was left of the old James Gang had gotten the blame for the Ellinwood holdup, but it had been the Shingletons instead. They'd gotten about five hundred dollars between them at Ellinwood, and they'd given that to their mother, who hadn't asked any questions.

Ma had never asked asked any questions, Billy told Cora. Not when the sheriff had come, not when her sons had disappeared for days or weeks on end, not when one or the other of them had come home nursing a wound. George had gotten himself shot twice in various scrapes, and never once had Ma asked where or why one of her boys had caught a bullet. Pa was dead and buried by then, and she was worn out from raising her brood on beans and flour gravy; if there was a few dollars extra in the old pickling crock in the cellar, then it was found money to tide them through the lean times that had always come along, and so not to be questioned. That had been her philosophy, and all her boys had been only too glad to go along with it.

Billy paused in the telling of his story and let it rest for a minute or two. Talking about Ma troubled him. Ma's silence about the money was the one thing he knew Cora wouldn't understand. He didn't himself. Some part of him had always wanted his mother to ask him about the money—to tell him that the stealing was wrong. That's what Cora would have done. He could tell she had principles. Not that his mother didn't. It was just that Ma had let life whittle away at her to the point she didn't care. Cora hadn't worn down that far. Not yet.

He looked at her in the silence, which was punctuated only

by the sound of the rain on the roof. Her big knuckles were working on one another as she held her hands clasped tightly in the praying way, as if she were hearing a testimony in church. He looked at her squarely, and his eyes told her that he should tell her no more for now.

And still her fingers worked against one another. The judging was going on for a long time.

"Why did you lie to me about your name?" she asked at last, as if that was the greatest sin he'd admitted. "Even after he came, when I asked, you said your name was Smith. I knew better all along, and you knew I did, but still you lied. If you'd have said Shingleton right off, the first time you rode into my yard, I'd have thought no different of it. Or of you."

"But what if he'd come the next day? Or if you'd of got word from the sheriff over to Wagon Mound or wherever that they were lookin' for a bank robber name of Billy Shingleton? What would you of done? Blast me with your shotgun to collect the reward?"

Even before her reaction registered, he knew he had gone too far. Her knuckles went white from the way she gripped them and the blood shot to her face.

"I'm no killer, Mr. Shingleton. No money on earth is worth killing for."

He tried to back out of his mistake.

"Well, I didn't know that, did I? And anyway, you wouldn't have lied for me."

She mulled over the truth of that for a moment. "No," she said slowly, "I guess I wouldn't . . . not at the first, anyhow. Not like I did tonight." She took a deep breath before the final accusation. "But then, I never would have taken you for a killer, either."

He couldn't bear the intensity of her gaze. He found himself looking at his hands, which to his surprise were clenched as tightly as hers.

"That's because I'm no killer, Cora," he said weakly. He

didn't think of himself as a killer, but perhaps the marshal was right. Perhaps he was. "If I ever shot anyone, it was in self-defense."

"Self-defense while you were robbing them of what was rightfully theirs?"

He shrugged and looked away.

"I think you better go, Billy," she said. The words came out more kindly than she'd intended. "Before that big man comes around looking for you again." She took a deep breath and held it, then said the last thing that needed saying. "Go before there's a killing on my place. His, or yours."

"You want me gone tonight?"

She considered it carefully, letting the very act of deliberation tell him more than he wanted to know.

"No, the morning will be soon enough," she said at last. "After it quits raining. But I want to be shed of you before that marshal comes back, you hear? And he will be back. I'll give you a mule because you've earned it. But I want you gone."

There was no recourse; he nodded in silent acknowledgment of her decision and tipped his head toward the door.

"S'pose he's waiting out there now?"

"He'd be a fool to sit out in this weather."

Billy rose and stepped across the little room. "He's been fool enough to follow me all the way from Kansas. Will you douse the light so's he won't see my silhouette against the door?"

She reached over and turned down the wick. Then he braced himself for the cold onslaught of the rain and stepped outside.

In the peculiar way the wind works in rain, he heard the horse go down without being able to tell where, or even in what direction. From the horse-sounds, it was a bad spill.

So there was no damned doubt that the marshal was still out there, although now he would be afoot. Or hurt. Hurt would be best, but Billy couldn't risk believing that, at least not right away. He knew that a man afoot was far more dangerous than a man on horseback struggling with a balky animal on a night like this.

Shingleton hunkered down alongside the house and waited. The rain sizzled into the rain barrel Cora had set out, and by squeezing himself up against it, he could make himself invisible to anyone sneaking around in the yard. He was wet to the skin and chilled, but vigilance and pure self-preservation meant that he'd wait for as long as it took to be sure he hadn't been seen.

Sometime later the horse stumbled into the yard. It was half-wild with fright. Cora heard the whinnying and came outside, armed as always with the shotgun and a lantern that didn't want to stay lit in the rain. She strode past Shingleton without seeing him, and he watched her as she followed the horse into the side yard and toward the corral. From his shelter alongside the rain barrel, he could see the little flickering pool of light move across the yard. He saw that she was brushing the horse, trying to comfort it. Then the lamp went out altogether.

In the darkness, he sensed that she was leading the horse past him, and at that moment a greenish white flash of lightning lit the yard and showed him in its glare what had happened.

The horse hadn't just gone down. The saddle was wrenched half off, and the animal was favoring a sore hind leg. Its back was smeared with mud and grass. Billy had seen enough spills to know that the horse had gone down hard and rolled, most likely with the rider underneath.

So Marshal Tom Alvarez was still out there and probably hurt.

Shingleton got up, letting the accumulated rain wash off him, though he kept an eye on the yard just in case Alvarez wasn't hurt that badly. As soon as the woman had tied up the horse and gone inside, he inspected it more closely.

The mare laid her ears back at his approach, but she was too played out to strike out at him. She nickered, and he patted her neck to gentle her. The cold, wet flesh twitched under his hand, and the horse shifted her weight off the favored foot. Whatever had become of him, Alvarez had nearly killed his horse this night.

Shingleton couldn't help but smile.

Something about this Godforsaken corner of nowhere makes a man abuse his horseflesh, he thought.

He rapped on the door and spoke Cora's name softly enough so no one else could hear, no matter how near they were. He had to repeat it twice before she heard.

This time, he couldn't resist a chuckle when the barrel of the twelve-gauge preceded her out the door.

"He's still out there, Cora," he said.

"I know that. I was getting a poncho to go look for him."

"He's probably hurt."

"I reckon. That horse took a bad fall."

He held out his hand. "Give me the shotgun. I'll go find him."

He saw the look on her face and she drew the gun back out of his reach.

"I told you I'm no killer, Cora. I just want it for protection. That's all."

"Just leave him alone then."

"And let him die, maybe? That ain't much different than killing him, is it?"

"Maybe it's a trick," she said, suddenly unsure of herself or the situation. "Maybe he's just waiting for you out there."

"You saw the horse. Now give me the gun."

"What'll you do?"

"Bring him in. Then I'll leave. In the morning."

Mistrust and confusion and fatigue clouded her face. He found himself thinking it was a handsome face despite all that, or perhaps because of it.

"Why should I trust you? If you want a gun, you have your own."

"It's black night and pouring rain," he said soberly. "If he tries to take a shot at me, I want to be able to shoot back. A man's got that right, at least. And a shotgun will make up for my eyesight in this weather. But I don't plan on doing anything except bringing him in."

There was a movement in her taut facial muscles, and then decision. She held the shotgun toward him. He took it, and before she could allow herself second thoughts, he had touched the brim of his hat in salute and turned and loped away into the rain.

It took Shingleton what seemed like a long time before he found Tom Alvarez, though he had no way of knowing just how long. The rain had let up a little, but the night had grown darker, if anything. Using the single light from the window as his anchor point, he swept back and forth across the southwestern corner of the Diemert place, just past the fence line. As he worked, he moved cautiously across the area where he thought the horse must have fallen. The going was rough in the waterlogged sand, and the tussocks of grass and flowing mud slowed him considerably. No wonder the horse had gone down.

Shingleton had almost given up when he found the spot where the horse had first stumbled, then had struggled to keep its feet. A few yards down the slope he found a deeper tearing, and then the man.

The horse had wallowed and slid, its weight actually driving its rider deep into the mire, and afterward the depression had filled with water, leaving the crumpled human body nothing more than an island in the middle of a small pool.

Shingleton leaned over Tom Alvarez and aimed the shotgun at his head just in case of tricks, but it was obvious that there weren't going to be any. The man was gasping for air and had one leg folded beneath his body at an impossible angle.

"Shit," Billy said softly. At the sound, Alvarez opened his eyes. He struggled a little, then the eyes slid shut again.

Shingleton thought he had passed out until the marshal grunted and tried to shift his weight again.

Billy cocked the shotgun and for a second considered pulling the trigger. Not to save himself, but to put the man out of his misery, just as he had killed his dying horse after the snakebite.

He didn't shoot.

Cora would know. There would have to be a burial, and in any case this was one killing she would not forgive. Men might kill horses to save them suffering, but they did not kill one another for the same reason.

"Damn you, Marshal, you surely complicate things!" This time he said it loudly enough to be heard over the drizzling rain. He let down the hammers and reached down to feel the twisted leg. Alvarez grimaced and tried to pull away, but the pain convulsed him.

"Don't seem the bone's pierced the flesh," Shingleton said as much to himself as to the lawman. He thought over his prospects for a moment, then trotted back to the house to collect bed slats and rags to make a proper splint.

It was crazy, this thing he was doing. Plumb crazy. Letting a widow woman get under his skin so that now he was going to have to nurse-maid a marshal who'd just chased him over five hundred miles of rough country. If they'd come upon one another in different circumstances, the confrontation would have ended quickly, with one the victor and the other the vanquished. There would be loaded weapons in Alvarez's saddlebags to attest to *his* intentions. The man was surely primed for killing. And Billy knew that he would not have hesitated to shoot as straight and true as he could to save his own skin, either. They were men prepared to accept violence as the price of their encounter.

The woman made it different.

"Bloody damnation!" the young man said. He saw a little pool of light flicker and move toward him as he approached the house. She was coming his way with the lantern.

"We've found him!" he shouted. "Now what in hell are we going to do with him?"

And so she sat, fumbling with the Bible. She found her Psalms and tried to read, but this night there was no comfort to be found.

CHAPTER 8

THE rains ended shortly before midnight, and the winds shifted to the north, blowing away the last trailing thunderheads and leaving the cold stars in their place.

The arroyos coming down from the foothills of the Sangre de Cristos were running bank-full and more, spilling over with the foaming silted water that rushed off the mesas. Along the South Canadian and its normally summer-dry feeder streams, pieces of bank strained under the weight of the water, cracked, broke, and plunged into the torrents, exposing yet more fresh earth to the hungry waters. The streams ate at the sand beneath the bunch grass, tore it away, and moved on; by morning, the floods had gone far toward carving out new channels all along the main river and its many tributaries.

Down the Canadian, where the riverbed was flat and broad, the rushing waters gathered in slow-moving wide brown pools on the plain and turned man-sized tufts of grass into islands that quickly drowned along with the clumps of prickly pear and cholla in the hollows. Snake holes and jackrabbit burrows flooded, drowning their occupants, and the fine sandy mud gouged up from the streams settled into the dens, sealing up the victims.

Cattle gathered in the low places to wait out the storm were swept off their feet by the rising water and sent bawling and thrashing into the current. They rolled their eyes and swam, but many grew exhausted and inhaled too much water, and in time they rolled onto their sides and floated wherever the water would carry them.

As the first grayness of dawn crept onto the world, a line

of pale blue slivered the pewter, separating earth from sky, and with it came a warmth that promised to burn away the last remnants of the storm. By the time the homesteaders and ranchers living on the Kiowa Plain had hitched up their galluses and gone out to do the morning chores and see what damage was done, the sky was mottled and rose and pungent with the sweet smell of wet saltbush and grama grass. Only the bloated rivers, ugly and choked with mud and brush and dead things, remained of the storm.

Cora Diemert arose early; she had been unable to sleep, anyway. Not with the strange man cursing with pain on her floor and another man—a killer, perhaps—asleep in the shed.

Her place had fared reasonably well in the downpour. A corner of the lean-to was threatening to collapse where the rain had undermined the footings, and some of the chickens were soaked and muddy. The runoff had scarred the grass and dug a little channel of crumbling sand where the yard sloped away from the big cottonwood. Some smaller branches had broken off the great tree, and she would be able to fill a bushel basket with the big leathery leaves that had blown down. But the grave was undisturbed, and everything else seemed to have survived the rain well. The bull snorted and pawed the soft earth at her approach, and the mules were braying as usual for their morning corn. Whether the seed herd out on the tablelands had done as well was something she'd have to look to later.

She fed her own livestock and only then went to see about Marshal Alvarez's horse, which was still saddled and tied by her door.

The animal looked so bedraggled that for a moment she feared it was dying. She stripped off the saddle and led it behind the house and hobbled it in the shade of the tree. Cora found a pan for cracked corn and a handful of oats, and while the horse snuffled and chewed the grain, she rubbed it down with a currycomb. The lame leg was tender but not swollen. She was no judge of injuries in animals, that had always been Henry's business; but though the horse favored the leg, it stood on all fours and seemed placid enough while she worked. It would survive, she reckoned; Marshal Alvarez had gotten himself into a far worse fix than his horse had.

When she finished her chores, she watched Billy Shingleton coming back on foot from the ridge where he'd found the marshal; even at the distance, she saw how the concern hung on him like a dead weight. She brushed a straggling strand of hair from her eyes and waited for him.

"You're up early," she called out to him when he was still thirty yards away.

"Arroyos are full of water everywhere. I'll bet the Canadian's a mile wide this morning, and quicksand every foot of the way."

She nodded.

"I've got to wait for the streams to dry before I'll be able to cross," he said simply, when he had come up to her.

A twinge of something like a combination of relief and regret made her shudder involuntarily; she did not know what she had thought he was doing this morning, but the fact that he was attempting to stay true to his word to leave pleased and saddened her at the same time.

"It happened once before like this," she said. "Last fall. Didn't rain this hard then, so I suppose you're right about the river." For all of Henry Diemert's failings, he had picked them a spot of decent ground that drained well enough to keep them from floating away at the first cloudburst.

Shingleton shifted his weight from one foot to the other and glanced over his shoulder toward the house. It was deathly quiet in the morning light—as still as if it were deserted. Only a faint wisp of gray smoke rose from the chimney.

"Well, I'd like to be on the move."

"Thank you for bringing him in last night," she said, intentionally failing to mention her own role in the rescue.

Shingleton's jaws tightened. "Can't let a man drown, can we?" He stumped off toward the shed but turned to face her again before he quite got there.

"I've got his guns, you know, and I aim to keep them. I saved his skin because you wanted it that way, but he'll have mine if I give him half a chance. I don't plan to do that, Cora. Not for you, or anyone."

"He's in no condition to have your skin, Mr. Shingleton. The man's delirious. I can't be sure he won't lose the leg or worse."

"Just the same, I'm watchin'. And I *will* be gone the first chance I get."

The stray hair fell in her eyes again and she brushed it away with the back of her hand. "I know you will, Billy. But it was a decent thing you did last night, just the same." She wanted suddenly to ask again about Kansas and his brothers and the Larned bank; she could not imagine this boy killing anyone, but she held her tongue, embarrassed by her own sudden softness. There would be another time.

He waved toward Alvarez's horse. "Wrap that leg tight and it'll be as good as new before long. Give it a chance to get some of the sweet grass around here, though I'd guess that animal's too used to oats for its own good." Then he was gone into the darkness of the shed, into the corner where she knew he'd hidden those saddlebags under a pile of straw.

"I reckon you're right," she said, long after he was out of hearing.

Too much needed doing, and so she would have to depend on others—on the children and on the young man. Cora Diemert was not used to depending on anyone, not even on Henry, who had taught her, after all, that it was her instincts and hard work that put the backbone in the family. So much to be done . . .

*   *   *

"Joseph, you take a mule and see how the rest of the cattle made it through the storm." She mopped the sweat from her forehead and went back to stirring the pot of bubbling porridge.

"Yes, Ma." The boy sat at the table, gobbling his corn bread.

"And don't try crossing any arroyos if there's still water in them. You'll get the mule bogged down in the mud for sure. If you can get to the cattle, fine. If you can't, leave 'em be. I'd rather lose some cows than you."

"Yes, Ma," the boy said again.

Cora stirred the porridge with a vigor that bordered on anger. It was far too hot a day for oatmeal, but the marshal would need something to stick to his ribs when he was ready, and oatmeal and molasses would stay with him for a long time. He had fallen into a sound sleep sometime while she was outside currying the horse, only to come to when she returned. For the last hour he'd been catnapping, and it was her intent to be ready to feed him when he came around again. The porridge boiled thick and slow, with deep sighs that sent little puffs of hot steam into the air around her face.

Tom Alvarez was propped up against the outside wall with the splinted leg thrust out in front of him. His muddy trousers were slit from the knee down to accommodate the bed slats, and his foot was bare where they had cut the boot off: it was swollen to twice its normal size and already an ugly blue-black. Cora had felt the broken bone slip into place when she'd set it the night before, but there was no telling how much of the soft tissue was torn inside, nor whether there might be some deep internal infection. He must surely be in great pain.

As she watched, his eyelids fluttered open and he sniffed loudly through the hawk nose to clear his head. Even from where she stood, she could see that his eyes were bloodshot and dull. Perhaps that was a good sign; she had seen enough dying to know that the gravest danger came when the eyes shone with the inner fires of fever.

"Do you want some coffee?" she asked.

He squinted at her and sniffed again. His lips parted and he licked them with a sleep-thickened tongue.

"I have porridge˙ cooking, but the coffee's ready now, Marshal."

"Yes," he said slowly. "Coffee." The voice was weak. He tried to move his bulk, and the sharp pain in the leg caught him up short and made him wince.

She poured the coffee in a tin mug and took it to him.

"We brought you here last night and splinted the leg best we could. You oughtn't move, though the bone's set, I'm sure. Your horse is outside."

He held the hot coffee to his lips and took a sip. "Thank you," he mumbled and drank again. The coffee was good. He sagged against the wall, but he kept his eyes fixed on Cora. Something she had said had struck him so that he had to struggle to think. And then he knew.

" 'We'? Who's 'we'?" he asked at last.

She took a deep breath before answering. She had expected the question, had even prepared an answer; but still the question, once asked, surprised her, and she felt faint of heart. She brushed the loose strand of hair from her eyes again and felt grateful for having something to fidget with for whatever small moment it would take to regain her composure. She wanted to lie to the marshal, even though he would know the truth before long. And what difference did the truth make, anyway? Anger welled up in her again— anger at Billy Shingleton for intruding on her in the first place, anger at herself for taking him in and for being taken in by him, and anger at this new intruder who had revealed the truth to her and thereby had threatened her peace in a way Shingleton never had and never would.

Yes, she would be truthful, because there was no reason to lie. Not to this man who was helpless before her.

Not to any man.

"I splinted your leg. A man named Bill Smith brought you down off the ridge. He has been staying here doing odd jobs for me. I believe his real name is Shingleton. The man you are looking for."

A half-smile crossed Alvarez's face, and he took a big gulp of coffee in self-satisfaction.

"God damn!" he said.

She reached out and snatched the coffee away from him, spilling most of it on the floor.

"You may *not* use that language in my home! I have children and will not put up with blasphemy!"

There was fire in her for this violation of her most sacred household rule, and even in his pain and drowsiness he rose to meet it.

"My pardon, ma'am," he said quietly. "I suppose your children are not perverted by the presence of a robber and murderer."

She whirled away from him; when she did it, her foot brushed against his injured leg. He bit down hard to keep from screaming at the pain, but like the coffee, it sharpened his senses. He reached for his gun instinctively, but of course it was gone.

So she holds all the cards, he thought.

"The oatmeal's ready," she said coldly.

"Then I'll take some."

When she handed him a bowl, he started to gulp the hot molasses-richened gruel; but the smell, at first so satisfying, was suddenly too rich, with what seemed to be the sticky sweetness of decaying flesh. On the second bite his stomach rebelled, and before he could stop the reflex, he'd vomited onto the floor beside him.

Cora Diemert glared at him, but she quickly scooped up a handful of rags and the soapy bucket of water she'd used for the morning dishes.

"I'm sorry," he said weakly, and he put down the porridge and allowed his heavy body to sag back against the wall.

She said nothing while she cleaned up his mess. When she finished, she took the bowl away but poured him some more coffee.

He sipped at it for a while, and when the cup was nearly empty, he moved so that he could stretch out full length on the floor. He missed the Smith and Wesson, but he sensed instinctively that in her angry way, she would protect him. She had set the bone and made him breakfast; Alvarez had work to do, but like her, he would take his time.

He slept again, with the throbbing in his leg only a distant annoyance.

Joe took the mule to the north pasture, above the place where the western ridge and the mesa turned away and disappeared onto an open plain marked only by the saltbush and the crosshatching of gullies like a giant haphazard spider web.

The flood waters were already subsiding; by the end of the day, the only reminder of the flood on the high ground would be the stagnant pools in the flats and the mud in the gullies. For now, though, where the water still flowed, it was thick and brown and carried the debris of the storm.

He found a few head of their cattle on the flats and a few more across one of the gullies. He followed the cut bank for some distance to see if there might be a place where he could cross. He didn't find a ford, but at one spot where another arroyo joined the first, he found something he was not prepared for.

At the point where the two washes came together, a whole section of bank had collapsed into the water, and something odd was sticking out of the wet sand and mud on the far side, where the current would have been weakest. At first, he thought it was only some cottonwood limbs washed downstream, but when he got off the mule and took a closer look from the edge of the arroyo, he recognized it for what it was—a cow. The water had washed the mud off the spot where she was branded; it was a Diemert cow. One hind leg and the stump of a broken horn stuck out of the sand crazily, like broken branches on the old sawyers that clogged the bigger rivers in the spring. Perhaps, once the sand dried, the head would reappear, but the rest of the animal was deeply buried, and would remain so unless the tawny plains wolves and the buzzards came in to pick over the carcass. The blow flies were already at work on the exposed flank.

Joe knew suddenly that there would be others—that the scavengers would feast well. Perhaps bunches of grazing cows had been swept away together along with their spring calves, to be found eventually in just such low-lying places as this.

His mind raced. What would he tell his mother. He knew she'd worry about whether there would be enough of the herd left to keep going.

And he thought of his father.

More than anything else, when Joe thought of his father, he thought of melancholy, of the profound sadness that seemed to envelop the man.

Joe remembered all the times his father had sat in silence on the wagon seat during their journey from the Indian Territory to New Mexico with eyes unblinking, fixed on the oxen as they plodded along across the Staked Plains. Joe had learned long ago that he couldn't talk to his father at those times; Henry was very far away from all of them when he got like that, as surely as if there had been a physical separation. Joe had seen the look on his father's face, and he had seen that other look on his mother's face as well—the look that said: *You've done this once too often, Henry. For the love of God, no more.*

His mother had never spoken those exact words, but Joe knew they were inside her. He'd never heard one word of argument pass between his parents when they thought the children were awake, but Joe had nonetheless overheard his mother sometimes in the deep of night when she had told Henry in no uncertain terms that his melancholy, his root-lessness, was destroying them.

Joe had heard, and he had remembered.

He remembered, too, that nothing had changed when they had stopped their wandering here. The same faraway look had come to his father's face when Henry sat in the shade of the cottonwood reading his seed catalogues, or when he would put down his spade in the middle of well-digging and sit for what seemed like hours and look with unseeing eyes across the breadth of the New Mexico plain. Joe remembered as well how his mother had looked at those times, with the tightness in her lips and the way she narrowed her eyes to watch her husband.

So he had decided there and then: Cora was the strength in the family, and Henry was the weakness. And Joe had found himself wondering about himself, wondering which of these two parents he was more like.

Joe missed his father, even though he was old enough to fully understand that it was Henry's crazy dreaming that had brought them to this place where his mother was so un-happy. He hated his father for that coldness the man had brought on his mother, and he hated him for leaving, for the quick death that had snatched him away just when the family needed his strong back the most. Yet, he loved him, too.

Joe took a last look at the buried cow and remounted the mule. He nudged it with his knees. He still needed to see if he could get across the arroyo to the living cows on the far side.

His father had died so suddenly. That was what made it so hard to understand, no matter how much he thought on it.

It had been early March. Calving time. Joe and Henry had gone out together to look after the cattle, to help pull calves if they were lucky enough to come upon heifers having a hard go of it. They'd been out all day in blustery weather and had found only one cow that needed help, and so they'd done what they could, with Joe sitting on the mule while Henry tied the rope to the pommel and to the forelegs of the unborn calf. It had been Joe's job to handle the reins, backing the mule up slowly while the rope snapped taut and pulled the calf. There had been elation for Joe in that work, a growing sense that he was somehow on the verge of manhood. And there had been the sense, too, that his father was proud of him, could look upon him and work with him without seeing the ghost of little Henry, the other son lost to the scarlet fever in Missouri—the great loss that Joe knew had started the hungry westward movement of their family.

They had gone home happy and tired and joking with each other that day. Only after they had gotten home, while they were rubbing down the mule together, had the father complained of a sudden stiffness in the neck and a headache. Joe had finished the chores while his father went to the house to rest, and by the time he himself went inside, Henry was gone.

Ma said Pa had just sat down at the table, gotten a nose-bleed, and died.

And Ma had changed after that day.

Joe tried not to think on it, tried not to recall what she had done that terrible night and the day after, but it was no use. The memories could not be held back. Not out here, alone on the plains, so close to new death.

And so he remembered.

How she had buried their father by herself, with the children watching as they huddled together beside the tree. That came to him in nightmares sometimes now. Nightmares and daydreams both.

Ma had dug the grave, laid him in it, said her good-byes, and filled it in and read from the Bible. By herself, summoning up some strength her son could only marvel at—and fear. And then she had gone back to the house to do the wash.

Joe felt the mule stop of its own accord.

He looked around. They'd gone some ways west, to a spot where they could cross the arroyo at last.

But they were no longer alone.

A hundred yards ahead, Bill Smith was leaning on a shovel—the very one Ma had used to bury Pa—and waiting for them to come on.

Bill raised his hand in greeting and dropped the shovel to roll a smoke while he waited for Joe to catch up to him.

CHAPTER 9

FRANK McAlester looked across the eight feet of blue smoke haze that separated him from Rawley Thomas. The boy was tying a jagged chunk of iron onto the end of a short black horsehair whip he had been braiding. Rawley had grown quiet these last days; the shaming he'd taken on that little squatter ranch west of the Canadian had set him to brooding. McAlester knew an embarrassment like that would almost always light the fire of vengeance in a man, but it was usually a reckless vengeance that burned too fast and too furiously. Rawley Thomas was a different sort. He was dwelling on the insult, all right, but the older man was content to let him brood.

McAlester took a slow pull off his cheap Mexican cigar and eased back on his bunk. Other men came and went with crude jokes and nervous laughter as they scrubbed themselves down and put on their best clothes for the supper being prepared for them in the sprawling big house on the hill, but McAlester and Thomas didn't move.

"Grub's damn near on, Frank," one of the cowboys said from the doorway. His long black hair was shiny from pomade and combed straight back, leaving a three-inch strip of white forehead above the wind-reddened face. The skin around his eyes was wrinkled like an old hide, and the eyes themselves were narrow and gray from too much looking into the sun.

"You go on ahead, Johnny. Me an' Rawley'll be along in a minute or two."

"Suit y'self, Frank. Jist don't blame me if all them oysters is gone. First come first served, ya know."

"I know."

"Well, hell!" Johnny giggled and hitched up his trousers and trundled away toward the big house, his walk clumsy from the Spanish heels on his boots and the awkward swagger of his bowed legs.

McAlester's mouth was watering—had been all day, the way the breeze carried the cooking smells down across the yard to the bunkhouse—but he didn't give in to it. He wanted to study Rawley some more. Still, the thought of that supper couldn't help but warm him.

This was the boss's way. A big feast before the long hard work of the roundup and the inevitable endless days of greasy beans and pan bread.

There would be feasting tonight, all right. The boss would see to it. Capons and mashed potatoes: a crisp, golden-skinned, fat chicken for each man. And snap beans from the garden the Miller women kept behind the house, and fresh yeast rolls and last summer's currant jelly. But best of all, there would be oysters. Whole fistfuls of the chewy meats swimming in the milky stew. Those oysters had come all the way from Louisiana by rail—bushels of them packed live in wet seaweed nestled on cakes of ice. All the way from New Orleans to El Paso, and from there up the trail in the freighter's wagon. Rumor had it that Rudy Miller had spent hundreds of dollars on those oysters, but then nothing was too good for his boys. Not now, at least, when they were getting ready to earn a year's pay all at once. Later, if the numbers didn't pan out, if they didn't scare up enough Box Elder stock or find enough unbranded calves to promise a fair shipment to the Chicago slaughterhouses next summer, then there'd be hell to pay, and a lot of good hands would get booted off the ranch with nothing to their names but whatever clothes they were wearing and maybe their saddles.

But for now, they were the princes of this kingdom and worthy of such treatment. That was the way it had been on the Miller place from the beginning, from the time when

Rudolph Senior had come into the country with John Chisum. The old man was dead now, laid to rest yonder in the family plot hard by the vegetable garden, but the son was carrying on where his father had left off.

Some of the boys didn't like facing sure firing if the pickings proved lean out on the plains, but others, the ones like Frank McAlester who had been around ten, fifteen years, did. As McAlester told them when they grumbled about the cruelty shown to cowboys who couldn't cut it, the Millers were in the business to raise cattle. Period. Their hired help was there solely to see to it that the herd grew and improved every year. The smart cowboy saw to it that the herd prospered. One way or another. And in payment, you could look forward to capons and oysters another year.

"You ready, Rawley?" McAlester asked at last.

"I guess."

"I don't mean for supper, boy."

The kid looked at him through the cigar smoke. His eyes looked to McAlester like black pinpoints in the sunburnt creases of his face.

"I'm gonna get that bastard for sure, Mr. McAlester."

"You will. But just remember why we're goin' up there again."

The kid half smiled.

"Sure. Miller cows."

McAlester bit off the end of the cigar and flipped the glowing butt through the open door. It landed in the dust to smolder out in its own good time. He chewed the rest slowly and deliberately, to get all the kick out of the tobacco before he went up to the house. The missus didn't permit spittoons in her dining room. That was the bad part about being foreman. The boys could eat in the yard, heaping their plates from long tables laid out in the shade of the elms old Rudolph had planted, but the foreman had to eat with the boss inside, off the china and silver. You didn't chew tobacco in there.

"You remember it, boy. Save the hate for the right time and place. When it will help you get Miller cows."

An hour later, McAlester settled himself into the cane chair on the broad, shaded veranda. The oysters and the meal and the wine had made him sluggish.

The boys were still sitting at the big tables, but they were smoking now and laughing easily while Josiah, the Negro cook, played his harmonica. The boss had set out some whiskey for them, enough for a couple of snorts apiece, but not so much as to make them drunk. In a little while, Rudy Miller's wife and daughters would pass among them with sweet cakes and wish them all luck in the roundup, and there might be a square or two of dancing for a time. Then they'd say their good-nights and wander down the hill to the bunk-house, each of them ready to do battle against the devil himself if necessary for this man and his family. And in the morning, before the first sliver of sun had raised itself above the eastern horizon, they'd gather the remuda and mount up and ride out, little groups working in every direction, but the main thrust going north, toward the lush grasslands along the Canadian where the Miller cows would be found.

They'd rope and count and brand and cull and herd for weeks, eating trail dust and smelling burnt hide and sweating men and horses and hearing cursing cowboys and bawling cattle the whole while. Some hands working the other smaller ranches would join in to help, though the help was really only a way of keeping one another honest in the count. Unbranded yearlings would be assigned to herds by percentage; if sixty or seventy percent of the branded cattle wore the Miller markings, then six or seven of every ten unmarked cattle would be shooed into the Miller herd. And if there were other cows and calves with strange brands—squatter's marks—the foremen would look the other way while the brands were altered and the animals distributed.

The squatters considered that theft, of course, but the

Millers and Chisums and their kind knew otherwise. It was war.

There wasn't enough grass for competition, not even in the good years. And when it was dry . . . well . . .

The big operators tolerated each other for a number of reasons. Blood ties, old friendships, respect born of fear. But the little herds, the new livestock springing up on the small ranches, were fair game the same as the fences the squatters dared put up around their places. If the newcomers could be discouraged into leaving, so be it. Cattle would be taken and fences torn down if necessary to assure the survival of the big ranches. When it took hundreds of acres to feed one cow and her calf in a wet summer and several times that in a dry one, no big operator could afford to lose so much as an acre of prime range.

McAlester had no illusions about why Rudy Miller had kept him on for so long. It was because he was good at rousting the squatters. After all, he'd been doing it ever since the old man had hired him—a green kid from Arkansas— for two dollars a month and board. But bigger challenges than they'd ever faced before lay ahead. If the newcomers pouring into New Mexico weren't driven out soon, there would be so many of them they'd stay and breed and stick; in time, even the cattleman's tool—the territorial assembly— would be powerless to root them out. Then the big outfits' days would be numbered. If McAlester and the others like him couldn't drive them off the land one way or another, then their own days would be numbered, too. The boss had made that clear even as they'd gobbled oysters and sipped the red claret that had come all the way from France.

Yes, Rawley Thomas had best hold the thought, keep the anger in check but seething just below the surface. For the proper time. For the time when they would go to the woman's place again.

Rudy Miller sat down in a rocking chair a few feet away. He was a smallish man with a red complexion and a soft, small mouth. Only the steel blue of the eyes and the strength in his hands displayed his true character.

"Lovely evening, Mr. McAlester. Best ever a man could want."

"That it is, sir."

"God has been good to me this summer. I trust he's given us a bounty of fat calves."

"Yes, sir."

Out on the lawn, Josiah had swung into a high-pitched and high-spirited rendition of "Dixie," and the boys were marching around the tables in step to the music. None of the boys had been in the war, of course; only a few, in fact, had even been born before Appomattox Court House, McAlester thought with a jolt. But they were southern men of southern stock, and the gentle reminders of the old glory (now but a faded, gilt-edged fable of a distant past) always cheered their hearts. The late afternoon sun cast a reddish glow on them all, and McAlester knew that the boss was right—it was a lovely evening.

"Indeed, God has been good to us here," Rudy Miller said, punctuating it with a self-satisfied belch. "Now it's up to us to husband what he's given us."

McAlester nodded in agreement and looked again toward the boys on the lawn. His thoughts drifted away from them quickly and came back to the woman on the little place up near the Canadian—the little woman who had driven them off twice now. They hadn't known her husband was dead the first time, and the second time she'd gotten some powerful help from a stranger; what, McAlester wondered, would a third visit bring? He felt sure deep in his bones that Rawley would need all that pent-up fury.

She was a force to be reckoned with. McAlester realized he respected her, even if she was a squatter intent on gobbling up the range that belonged by the right of first claim to the Millers and Chisums and the rest. So many of the other squatters had scared easily, especially in the early days when they were few. They'd turned white and quaking at the threats and hadn't fought back. Usually all it took was throwing a rope around one of the men and dragging him through a patch of prickly pear; if more persuading was needed, setting fire to an outbuilding would do.

But not with her. She had been ready for them the first time they'd come, driving them off with the shotgun. And now she'd gotten help from somewhere.

She had pluck enough to stand up to any man.

That was why McAlester admired her. And that was why he knew that, in the end, they would have to kill her.

"Have another drink, Mr. McAlester?" Miller said.

"No, thank you, sir."

"We'll have a good roundup, will we not?"

"We will, sir."

Miller grinned, and his eyes gleamed coldly in the glow of the setting sun. "Yes, I believe we will."

CHAPTER 10

HE rolled the smoke slowly, lit it, and handed it to Joe.

"Go ahead, boy. Give her a try." He was at his ease now that the digging was finished. He'd found a suitable place along the bank where a few cottonwoods grew. The rains and the swollen, rushing arroyo had not disturbed the sod; it would do well. That was why he'd chosen the place to bury the saddlebags.

"Come on, Joe. Give her a try!"

He was cool and strong now, almost cocky—what Cora Diemert would call a braggart—and it gave Joe a peculiar feeling to know that this man could be so different with him than with his mother. Joe had heard a great deal the night before while they thought he was asleep. When first the mule had brought him here, he'd been afraid that Smith—or Shingleton or whatever his name was—would think he was spying and dispatch him the way bad men dealt with by-standers who caught them in a criminal act; but Billy had gone right on burying the saddlebags without giving him so much as a cross look. And now that it was done, the man was offering him a smoke the way men did to companions who had shared a piece of work.

Joe reached out and took the offered cigaret. Slowly, he put the twisted paper to his lips and inhaled.

Tears came to his eyes instantly, and his lungs and throat rebelled even before he had a sense of the taste of the tobacco. Billy Shingleton gave him a strong, dark look that was almost violent yet had a hint of humor underneath.

"Smoke it, boy. All of it!" he commanded.

Joe took another drag on the cigaret and held the smoke in his lungs until they exploded.

Billy growled once and tried to growl a second time, but the growl melted into a chuckle and a rippling smile spread out across his face. He laughed out loud. "You like the taste of that cigaret?"

Joe took another drag on the smoke and did better at it this time, even though it made him lightheaded. He only coughed a little. Billy reached out and took the cigaret back and put it in the corner of his mouth while he laughed. A little curl of gray smoke wound around his nose and collected under the brim of his hat. Billy gave Joe a good-natured poke on the shoulder.

"You keep a secret, boy?" he asked after a time.

Joe nodded. His legs were rubbery beneath him and his ears buzzed as if he were caught in a mess of hornets. He had never imagined that anything could be as awful as the cigaret; he was glad that Billy had taken the smoke and awed that the man liked it. The two of them mounted.

"That's good that you can keep a secret. You don't tell about what I just done, and I won't tell your momma you were out here havin' a smoke." And he laughed again.

The boy grinned and shrugged.

Shingleton took a deep drag on the smoke until the red coal nearly burned his lips, then he flipped the butt into the mud along the arroyo. "Well, someday you'll like a smoke once in a while, but you've got time yet."

They rode for some distance in silence.

"What were you doin' out here, boy?" Billy asked at last.

"Ma sent me to look after the cattle. To see how many we lost in the storm."

"And how many did you lose?"

"Don't know. Some for sure. I seen one dead one."

"I saw some of your momma's cows and calves on the way out here. Looked fine to me."

"I seen some, too." Joe took a deep breath and plunged

ahead with the question he both feared and had to ask now that the two of them were conspirators, at least in the matter of cigarets. "What were you burying in them bags, Mr. Smith?"

Shingleton frowned but didn't hesitate to give Joe the answer he'd already rehearsed.

"Something that belongs to me. Something important. Let it go at that. And remember—you keep the secret."

Joe felt the blood rush to his face. He'd said he would keep the secret, all right, but it would be tough not even knowing what he secret was.

"I will."

"Swear?"

"Swear."

"Good." Shingleton grinned again. "You want a shooting lesson?"

"Reckon Ma wouldn't like that. She says I ought to learn to use the shotgun, but I don't think she takes to them pistols."

"What she don't know won't hurt her."

"She'll hear."

"We're two miles or more from the house. If she hears— and I doubt she could—I'll just tell her I was shootin' snakes."

"All right," Joe said. "Let me hobble the mule."

The two of them rode back in silence. Joe's hands and arms were sore from the kick of the Colt's and he had a taste like burnt biscuits and metal in his mouth from the smoke. All in all, he was satisfied. He'd forgotten the dead cow and the melancholy that had swooped down on him when he had found it. This Billy was a regular fellow; they had some secrets to share even if Joe didn't quite know what they were, and he promised himself he'd keep a watch out on the marshal to make sure the big hawk-nosed man left his friend alone.

Still, a stray thought nagged at him as they rode.

"You leaving soon, Mr. Smith?" Joe asked after a while.

"Why?"

"I just thought maybe you were."

"Soon. Maybe when the gullies dry out. I'm taking a mule. Your momma gave me one of 'em."

"Yessir. I heard."

"You did, huh?"

Joe looked at Billy and saw that his face had turned ominous again. "Yessir."

"Then what else did you hear?"

Joe hesitated for only a moment. "Everything, I guess."

"Well." The man lowered his voice to a whisper, and this time there was real menace in it. "Then you just keep that secret, kid. If you know what's good for you."

Billy Shingleton stayed away from the house for what was left of the day. Cora Diemert brought him a pan full of biscuits and milk gravy toward evening, and he ate alone in his corner of the shed while the chickens squawked and blustered themselves to sleep on their roosts nearby.

He felt as if his mind was paralyzed, unable to make a decent plan, and that troubled him.

The boy was no threat. He liked the boy, and after all, the kid had sworn: he would keep his mouth shut about burying the saddlebags. Nevertheless, a smart man would get on that mule and ride out of this place. Fast. The arroyos would be drying already, and Shingleton could be all the way to Las Vegas in less than two days. He'd rather take Tom Alvarez's big horse than a balky mule, but the horse was still drawn up lame. Maybe that was why he waited in spite of his own best judgment, he told himself. To give that big horse a chance to strengthen. If that horse was healthy, it could carry him all the way to wherever he wanted to go. Besides, Alvarez was out of action for a good long while, so what was the hurry?

Still, a smart man would get going. To Mexico, maybe. If George was dead and Danny had squealed to save his own hide, there would be no reason to head for the rendezvous they'd planned for Durango, across the main rib of the Rockies in Colorado. And even if the marshal was lying, even if his brothers were waiting for him there already, maybe it was time to think of himself first. A smart man could live very well for a long time in Mexico on the money in those saddlebags.

No doubt about it. A smart man would shoot Tom Alvarez dead as a precaution, dig up those bags, take one of Cora Diemert's mules just far enough to steal a decent horse, and head straight for Mexico. He'd have to swing west of El Paso, but he reckoned the law would be looking for him up north. If Alvarez had been looking north, so would the others.

Shingleton hunkered down in the shed to think.

A smart man would do all those things, all right. But a smart man wouldn't have buried that money. You couldn't make a quick getaway if you had to go looking for the damn saddlebags. Yet, it was good that he'd taken those saddlebags out on the plain and buried them. He knew that. But why? Why hadn't he done it long before now? Mostly, why did it seem the right thing to do now, just when by rights he should be getting ready to get away from this miserable little good-for-nothing ranch stuck in the middle of nowhere? He sure didn't owe Cora Diemert anything. Not now. Any debt he might have owed her had been paid in full by hard sweat over the last couple of weeks, if not by his gun when he'd driven off those cowboys. And how had she thanked him? By taking in the marshal, by nurturing and protecting the very man Shingleton had been trying so hard to keep ahead of.

"I should of killed him," Shingleton said aloud. The chickens stirred at the sound, and one of the roosters let out a halfhearted cock-a-doodle-do. Shingleton rolled a cigaret and smoked it down all the way before he let himself think on this thing again, for even in the back of his mind, he knew what direction his thoughts would take in spite of his best conscious efforts.

There was some invisible force that tied him to this hard-scrabble place, to this woman and her scrawny children.

That was it, of course. The woman and her children. So like his own Kansas family.

In spite of himself, he couldn't help a sardonic laugh. No, these people weren't like his own family at all, though deep inside he wished that his people had been more like the Diemerts. These children were polite and hard-working in ways he and his brothers never had been, and he knew they had gotten plenty of love, along with firm discipline. His own mother had been too worn down to give her boys the back-of-the-hand guidance they had so richly deserved from time to time, and his pa had been . . . well, the old man had never been much more than a worn-out drunk.

Shingleton had seen the way Cora bridled at the mention of her husband's name; from the way she clenched her fists or turned her head at those times, he'd long since guessed that she had grown disappointed in her man, especially since he'd up and died on her and left her out here in the middle of nowhere. But in spite of the disappointment, there was a flash of pride in her eyes when she spoke of him, too. Henry Diemert had died while he still had his wife's love, if not respect.

That, surely, was something his own father hadn't had. By the time his old man had died, drowning in his own vomit, his wife had been so used up that she hadn't shed a tear. Lord, she had only gone to the cemetery because the boys had pleaded with her.

So why was it that he saw something of his mother in Cora Diemert? Was it homesickness? A wish that he could go back to his own childhood and somehow make it all come out differently? Or was it just weariness, the bone-tiredness that had made him so willing to hole up here in the first place?

He lit another cigaret.

Maybe he wasn't cut out for bank robbing. Maybe he had

never been cut out for the fast life that had been so beguiling to his brothers.

The Lord knew it had sure seemed easy at the time. Something a kid had to do to keep up with his older brothers.

Dan had been wild from the start, but not nearly so wild or unpredictable as George. Dan was younger and devious, the one capable of stirring up trouble to the boiling point, then stepping back in time to leave his brothers with the blame for the mischief. George was a fighter, and to be honest, he wasn't very bright. Billy could remember the times he'd seen George going at it with fists and knees and teeth just for the pure fun of it. Dan had learned to use his older brother's energy early on, first against little Billy and then later against their father and others outside the clan. The old man used to whip them with a razor strap when they were little. If he'd been drinking, and he usually was, he would raise welts on their backs purely for the hell of it, but when the boys were old enough to team up against him, that had stopped.

One day when the father was chasing after Dan with the strap, the boy had screamed for George's help, and before the fight was over, the old man had lost three teeth and gotten a broken nose. After that, the drinking got worse but the beatings let up. Because George was such a scrapper and because Dan always urged his brother on, none of the Shingleton boys had many chums; it was only natural that they would become a little gang unto themselves.

Thinking back on it, Billy knew when it had begun in earnest, when they had turned mean. Their pa had been the excuse, if not the reason.

One night, a neighbor had brought their father home dead drunk and had proceeded to lecture Ma on the evils of drink. Dan, overhearing, had plotted revenge for this embarrassment. In the plan, Billy was to be the decoy and George the executioner.

They bided their time, waiting for the ill feelings between the families to ebb away, at least on the surface. Then, one summer night when heat lightning shimmered in the distance, the time was right at last. Billy went running to the neighbor's place to say that Pa had disappeared and maybe fallen down the well so please come quick to help get him out. The neighbor had saddled his mare and come.

Dan and Billy had combed the place alongside the neighbor while George, alone, hiked cross-country with a bucket of coal oil under his arm.

The swift little storm, full of lightning but no rain, had moved over the land before the neighbor gave up the search with the boys; and by the time he had gotten home, his barn had burned to the ground. None of his people could say for sure that something other than lightning had set the fire, so he'd had to let it go, but there had been bad blood between him and the Shingletons from that night on. And his place had been the first they'd ever robbed, looting it for silverware when he'd left the county to attend a funeral in Salina.

Yes, that was the start of it, the first realization that good money could be had by taking it from other people. By the time Billy turned fifteen, the brothers had worked themselves into a large, loosely knit gang of drifters with some old-time Kansas hands thrown in who met the brothers one place or another when either of the elder Shingletons had decided on a job. They made the circuit of central Kansas, occasionally beating up some perceived enemy or burgling his home.

Their pa had known all about it since some of his cronies were in the gang, but the old man was too smart to tangle with his older boys, and so he'd taken to screaming at Billy. Dan and George had only laughed at it, and in time so had Billy; after all, the old man hadn't the nerve to touch the strap again. From then on, their favorite sport on a winter's evening became finding ways to water their father's whiskey.

There hadn't been much trouble with the law, either. Not in the beginning, anyway. The town marshals or the county sheriffs had their hands full enough with murders to be more than anxious to overlook a little gang of toughs. Besides, the lawmen were in the pay of the cattlemen's association or the railroads, and if the gang left the big-money boys alone, the law would just as lief look the other way. They hadn't even cared much about the first serious holdup in Garden City. It was a German druggist, after all, and those foreigners were often as not troublemakers and fair game for good, red-blooded American boys.

George had been the bagman while Dan and Billy held the horses on that one. The old German was known for keeping cash on hand, and it hadn't taken much of George's muscle to pry it loose. The druggist was plenty glad to part with his money in exchange for keeping his teeth. The take had come to over two hundred dollars—more than enough to pay for a high time in Wichita they'd all remember for a long time. But it had been Dan who had said to save the money. They'd wait for the good times until they'd taken the Larned bank. There would be other robberies first, to get their plan worked out, but always the goal should be the Larned bank—the place that had ruined their father.

Funny, looking back. Billy and his brothers saw their dead pa as a worthless bum, yet his pain over the Larned bank was more embarrassing to them than anything else in their lives.

They'd had some trouble holding the gang together in those days. Two were gunned down in a poker game that featured some clumsy cheating and too much bad rye whiskey. Another, a drifter they'd known only as Si, simply disappeared, and one or two more decided to pick up stakes and head west to hook up with Butch Cassidy and the Hole-in-the-Wall Gang or some other bunch. One young kid even took a job as a town marshal down in south Texas someplace, but they'd heard a few months later that he'd been shot to death over a whore his first day on the job.

In spite of the shortage of manpower, they'd hit a small grangers' association bank in Ellinwood in central Kansas while they planned Larned, and finally the law did take an interest. Someone important had gotten burned and had brought in the Federal Marshal Service. The boys had laid low and clung to home. For the first time since they burned down their neighbor's barn, they had found it wasn't safe to ride into town on their own.

Instead, they had to sneak around in the middle of the night, and then only when there was no moon. Once, George got into a ferocious little gunfight when some lawmen set an ambush on the road a mile from ma's house. George got himself winged, but from the blood they'd seen in the road the next day, he'd wounded at least one of the lawmen, too. For once in his life, though, George had had the presence of mind to head for town and ride north from there for some miles before doubling back down a creekbed. It had thrown the marshals off, or so it seemed at the time; they'd given up on the boys and blamed the Ellinwood bank on the old James Gang.

Looking back now, Billy guessed that the marshals had known all along it wasn't the Jameses. They must have been just laying back, waiting for the boys to make a mistake.

No matter what the law thought, it wasn't long after the smoke cleared on Ellinwood that the boys decided they were ready for Larned.

It was a botched job from the beginning, in spite of all the planning they'd done.

Since Larned was known to be a tough bank to rob, Dan had hired a couple of young cowboys who'd been booted off a trail drive to hold their horses and keep an eye out. But these cowboys were skittish troublemakers who hadn't been seasoned by really tough scrapes. Their tempers were terrible, and more than once on the way to Larned, Billy had thought that Dan was going to kill them himself. Looking back, it might have been better if he had.

On the day of the robbery the cowboys were supposed to warn the brothers inside the bank if any trouble came up, but they'd shared a bottle over breakfast, and when the gun-toting old town constable had showed up bellowing and wheezing like a ten-year-old bull in rut, they'd forgotten everything. There wasn't supposed to be any shooting, but there was—and the gang was supposed to get away clean, but they hadn't. The horse-holders had bolted when the consta-ble fired a warning into the air, and Billy had had to dodge along the alleys around the bank until he could find a horse to steal to get away.

Dan and George had stayed behind, shooting. Before he'd even cleared the door of the bank, Billy had seen the consta-ble fall dead, but he hadn't known the fate of his brothers nor guessed that there had been a second victim until he'd heard the words from Tom Alvarez's lips. All he'd thought of at the time was their plan—to get to the western slope of the Colorado Rockies with the money, to make their rendez-vous out of reach of the Kansas law.

Now there wasn't to be a rendezvous.

At least not if Alvarez could be believed. If he was lying, if both brothers were alive and free . . .

Billy lit another smoke and inhaled deeply. In his bones, he believed the marshal was telling the truth. Maybe the smart thing to do would be to dig up the money and go to Mexico.

Colorado or Mexico. Which was it to be?

Or, maybe a smart man would just sit down and wait it out for a while, until he could get Marshal Alvarez away from Cora Diemert's place. A smart man would fix it so he wouldn't have to worry at all.

Well, that was foolish. Alvarez had been the hardest one to shake, but there would be other lawmen. That was a cer-tainty.

And as always, a part of the decision came back to Cora. The woman exasperated him, made him feel like a child who had done wrong. He resented her for that; and yet, she was a proud, strong woman who raised feelings deep inside him he'd never known before. She was someone a man couldn't boss or bother, a woman to be respected and reckoned with. He felt a deep need to help protect her, which confused him. Sometimes Cora made his heart pound, and not like the silly girls from home, either. That had been rutting lust, the way a body got heated up over full pink lips and the maddening smell of warm flesh. This was partly that, but something entirely different, too.

So maybe he'd hang around for a while, at least until Alvarez could be dealt with one way or the other.

"Damn!" he said out loud. He snuffed out his cigaret and went outside. There was no trace of daylight left in the sky, which had taken on a blackness he could almost feel. The Milky Way, cold and white, divided the blackness in two. The plains air was fragrant, filled with the heavy musk of saltbush invigorated by the rains of the day before. The grass would be lush and emerald green soon, and by tomorrow or the next day, the summer wildflowers would explode in a frenzy of life among the grasses while the ground was still soft and wet enough to nourish them.

He stood for a long time, listening. The bull belched and snorted and shifted its weight around as it settled down for the night. If he waited, concentrating, he could pick out the separate sounds of the night, the chirping of the crickets, the soft buzz of mosquitoes coming out of the newly washed gullies, the click of beetles as they crawled out of the grass for their night patrols, the soft wing-sounds of the bats.

From inside the house, he heard laughter. One of the girls was laughing with the high-pitched glee that only children can find within themselves.

"Damn," he said again, but this time softly. He went to the cottonwood to relieve himself before he settled down to sleep. This night, as always, he would keep one hand on his revolver. But tonight his saddlebag-pillow was elsewhere.

CHAPTER 11

TOM Alvarez pulled himself up slowly, using the chair back as a sort of lever and crutch to get his bulk off the floor and into a standing position. The leg throbbed all the time, but at least the throbbing meant that there was life in it; what he had feared most was the numbness that came with gangrene. Sensation in the foot meant that blood still circulated there, and circulation meant that, with luck, he would keep the foot even if it never worked quite the same again.

He managed to stand, but all his weight was on his sound leg and his arms as he leaned against the chair. Perspiration from the great effort trickled out of his thick mop of hair and stung his eyes. He tried to take a step, but the broken leg would not respond and he nearly fell. Sharp pain shot up his leg into his lower back as if someone had stabbed him with a hot knife above the kidney. He caught at the chair again and rested on it, suddenly aware of how precarious his balance was. One of the small children could have pushed him over. He had to remind himself to breathe deeply, not to give in to the pain until the spasm had passed. He had too much to try to do and too little time to do it in; if he got careless and passed out, all his plans would be futile.

After a few moments, the sharp stabbing pain subsided into a constantly throbbing ache that was with him always.

Alvarez looked around for his guns. The woman had hidden them where they couldn't be seen from the pallet he'd occupied this last three days, but he sensed they were close by. He had hoped that once he'd regained his feet, he'd find them within easy reach.

The woman was obviously too smart for that, and now he

was angry with himself for even thinking she could be so stupid. Of course she wouldn't make it easy for him; he would have to steel himself to hobble across the little house to the curtained-off sleeping area, and he would have to be quick about it. This was the first time the woman had left him alone, and she'd be back soon. She'd only gone to supervise the hoeing, to crack the whip a little over her children to see that they got their chores done. And, perhaps, to look in on Billy Shingleton.

When he considered the possibilities, Alvarez couldn't help being amazed that he was still alive. If the roles had been reversed, if he had been the killer being stalked and the lawman doing the stalking had chanced to have a serious accident . . .

Well, it amazed him.

Once again, he pushed himself upright and carefully put weight on the bad leg. The splints held it stiff enough to keep it from buckling beneath him, but the pain washed over him like a consuming wave and threatened to drown him. He'd had broken bones before, but never like this. Somewhere inside the leg something was wrong, some muscle was lacerated, a nerve pinched or torn. Perhaps there would be no gangrene, no requirement for amputation, but he knew the leg would never completely heal. Forever after, Tom Alvarez would be a cripple.

He worked at pushing the thought away from him. It took a hard physical effort to concentrate on what was more important for now. He had to find his guns.

He gritted his teeth until he thought his jaw itself would crack as he struggled toward the curtained room. He pushed the chair ahead of him, using it as a crutch. The place was small enough that he could move from the table to the stove to the rocking chair where the Diemert woman spent her evenings without overtaxing his strength. Beyond her chair was an ancient bureau that had apparently suffered greatly in the trek west; and just beyond that, within easy reach, was a coat rack, an oak board with stout pieces of dowel hammered securely into the wall. From there, he could reach the curtains. At each step, he took a few deep breaths and leaned on the chair back to take the strain off the leg.

When he got to the coat rack, he let go of the chair and hung onto the dowels. He desperately needed to rest. He tried to swing his body around so he could half-fall and half-stride into the chair. His heart was pounding so hard he could hear his pulse throbbing in his ears. He gave up on sitting and decided to finish what he had begun.

Only when he turned to try to cross the last few feet separating him from the curtains did he see that the door had swung open.

Shingleton was standing there alone, his gun visible but tucked into the top of his trousers.

Alvarez smiled through clenched teeth.

"Gettin' around, Marshal?" Billy said coldly. He rested a hand on the butt of the revolver.

"Trying," Alvarez said. He knew his voice was weak, but he tried hard to keep it calm and detached. Still, it came out too breathy. He had used himself up crossing the room. Little pinpoints of blackness began to swim in his field of vision and he suddenly wanted very badly to lie down.

"You won't find your guns, Marshal," Billy said with a smile. "We buried 'em."

Alvarez tried to answer, but nothing came out of his mouth. The black dots swam faster and faster and his ears began to buzz, and suddenly there was nothing but warm empty blackness engulfing him.

Cora Diemert sat in her chair with her Bible while the children talked quietly among themselves in their beds. Marshal Tom Alvarez was propped up on his pallet sipping quietly at what was left of the supper coffee. He had awakened from his faint to the smell of frying salt pork and corn bread, and his first sensation had been wonderment—once again—that he was alive at all.

The kid had had a second chance to kill him, but had not. The woman had been somewhere else; they had been alone in the place. Shingleton could have killed him easily, without any interference from her. But here he was alive and awake; except for feeding him, Cora was ignoring him completely.

So Alvarez drank his coffee and watched the children.

The boy Joe was trying very hard not to be seen looking at this crippled stranger, and once or twice he went to his mother to whisper something in her ear. No matter how hard Joe tried to appear nonchalant, his fascination with Alvarez was written all over his face. The girls, who were younger and more innocent, stared frankly sometimes as if he were a freak in a tent show, but their attention span was short; after a while, they just ignored him altogether.

They were pretty girls, given to the peculiar mix of boundless energy and shyness that seemed to go with their age. The boy already had a mannish look to him, and it was disturbing to see it on someone so young. He wore the responsibility like a heavy garment that would wear him out from its very weight.

Alvarez took another sip of coffee and felt his leg. The swelling had returned, probably because he'd been foolish enough to try to walk on it. Still, it might have felt a whole lot worse. The splints had probably saved him from hurting it further in the fall he'd taken when he passed out. His biggest problem now was that he had to urinate.

"I must relieve myself, ma'am," he said after he'd cleared his throat loudly enough to break Cora Diemert's self-imposed isolation within her Bible. He said it again and tapped a knuckle on the chamber pot beside him, just in case she missed the message when it took her a moment to look in his direction.

"I'm sorry, ma'am. Truly I am."

"Yes, of course." She rose and stepped behind the curtain by the beds and ordered the children to follow. She held the curtain closed with one fist behind her, a gesture that wasn't lost on Alvarez.

Protecting the innocent eyes of her children, no doubt. And, perhaps, shielding his eyes from the place where he might find his weapons.

He pulled the rag-covered chamber pot to the best spot and propped himself up on his good knee. When he'd finished, he called out to her that it was all right to rejoin him.

She returned to her book and the children to their staring, but after a few minutes, Cora put the Bible down.

"I've told Mr. Smith to make you some crutches so you can get yourself out to the privy. I'll not clean up after you forever, Marshal." She seemed to be looking off into space, past him.

"Thank you, ma'am. It would be a blessing for me as well. And may I ask whether Mr. *Shingleton* is doing as you asked?"

"Of course. Why?" She ignored his emphasis on the name.

"Because he could have killed me this afternoon, and he didn't. I think he wanted to, but he didn't. I wonder if it was because you have asked him not to."

She blushed crimson, and this time her eyes flitted into and out of his piercing gray gaze as if she feared it.

"Mr. Smith is no killer, sir," was all she said as she kept her eyes averted.

"But Billy Shingleton is, Mrs. Diemert. At least his brothers were, and in the eyes of the law, so is he. I'm in no position to fight him now, and I'm in no position to chase after him if he were to run again. You know that, and so does he. Still, I'm sworn to bring him in, and he knows that, too. Killing me makes a lot of sense. Yet he leaves me alone and stays on here in this place. I wonder why."

"Perhaps he isn't the evil man you suggest."

"And maybe he's just lying low, waiting to pick his time.

And getting certain . . . benefits . . . into the bargain." He said the words slowly, letting them fall into the distance between them.

Her eyes flashed, and the color came back into her cheeks, this time in anger, but she said nothing at all.

He sipped his coffee again and chuckled a little, though if pressed he couldn't truly say why.

The crutches were heavy and prone to giving him splinters, but they did make it possible for him to move around the yard. He came to enjoy his time outside in the sun; he'd never been one to let the sun fall on uncovered skin, but now the sunshine seemed to strengthen and warm him deep inside. And he could think better outside for some reason. Perhaps it was the fresh air, or just getting up off the pallet so the blood could circulate in his legs and buttocks properly. In any case, he was left free to move around as he chose. Shingleton avoided him as much as possible, and when they did see one another, they exchanged no greeting at all.

Alvarez made it a point to get a look at the little place Shingleton had fixed up for himself in the shed. The young man stood guard sometimes, but there were other times when Alvarez was going to or coming from the privy that he could see inside. *If* Shingleton had the money with him, Alvarez guessed that it was hidden somewhere in that shed. Used it for a pillow, probably, and hid it under some straw in the daytime. From what he could see from the doorway there wasn't much to the furnishings. A blanket, a saddle, and a coal oil lamp were about the only things visible from the doorway. There was a scabbard with the saddle, so Alvarez knew that Shingleton had a long gun somewhere, but that was hidden along with the money, probably just covered with the straw that the kid had piled along the back wall. He would have loved an opportunity to dig around in the place, but the young outlaw was never very far away, and he was always well armed. Even though the kid had passed up a chance or two to do him in, Tom Alvarez had learned from long experience that it didn't pay to tempt fate too often. Besides, he still had no idea what Cora Diemert had done with his own weapons.

He could bide his time, after all. He didn't have much choice in the matter, and besides, there would have to be a confrontation soon enough. One way or the other, Alvarez would get his hands on a gun, and then it would be time to take Billy Shingleton into custody and begin the long ride back to Kansas to make him pay for his crimes.

Somehow.

As he went hobbling around the dusty yard, Alvarez laughed bitterly as he thought about it. He'd been in a lot of tough scrapes over the years, but he'd always been tougher and meaner and better prepared than his opponents. Now it took all his strength to drag himself out of the house to the privy. Even though the leg was already beginning to mend, it would still be a long time before he could ride horseback for any distance. Once he got the drop on his prey, he'd have to commandeer the Diemert's buckboard for the trip to Las Vegas, then hire a seat on the Atcheson, Topeka, and Santa Fe; eighty miles of hard country was going to be tough riding for a man with a throbbing leg and a crafty prisoner who'd have to be watched all the time. Maybe the best thing to do would be to shoot Shingleton stone dead and just take the body back. There shouldn't be an inquest; this boy was charged with murder and a marshal had the authority in any case. Alvarez had never done a killing just to make things easier; but if ever there was a time, this was it.

And that assumed that he could get the drop on Shingleton, that Cora Diemert wouldn't interfere, or even that Shingleton wouldn't just high-tail it one of these mornings, leaving Alvarez alone with this ranch woman and a broken leg.

Ever a practical man, Tom Alvarez considered the odds and mulled over all the possible actions and their consequences. The odds were definitely against him. The cold light of reason told him that he, and not the kid, was the one most likely to be buried in some wash or left to the buzzards before this thing was over. He'd already taken to sleeping with one eye open, as he had in his younger days before creeping middle age and modest prosperity had made him a little lazy, but he'd have to keep both eyes open from now on; the hostility between himself and Shingleton was sure to burst into the open soon.

The marshal was the one who was going to have to make the move, and any chance of success depended on moving swiftly—and upon Cora Diemert.

The woman seemed to be losing patience with both men. More than that, she acted as if she expected the trouble that both were surely planning. Alvarez noticed she'd taken to carrying her shotgun when she went to do the chores, and she was keeping her children away from the marshal entirely. Shingleton was another matter: the boy Joe had plainly taken a shine to Billy. And it was clear the place needed man-work done, so she let Shingleton and the boy work together to get the wood chopped, the windmill repaired and greased, and the fences mended. The only comfort for Alvarez was that she was uneasy about it; that much a blind man could tell without even speaking to her.

The tension in her was nearing a breaking point. Her jaw muscles were knit tight, her eyes squinted in thought and worry every night. Alvarez tried to play on that, reminding her how Shingleton had been a part of a gang of killers and robbers, how he was not to be trusted. She responded to him not at all, but he saw it working on her, eating away at her confidence, and whenever he'd finished with his arguments, she'd turn to her Bible for solace and guidance.

Well, Alvarez thought, if it's really the Good Book, it'll tell her to do the right thing. Just so the right thing meant helping him!

At the end of the first full week of his convalescence on the crutches she came to him and told him that she would be moving him to the shed, to sleep in the place where Billy Smith slept.

It was time for a roundup, or as much of a roundup as one man and a boy could accomplish. Cora told him pointedly in a tone that brooked no interruption that the next day Joe and Billy Smith, as she still insisted on calling him, were taking a mule and Alvarez's horse out onto the open grasslands to look for Diemert cattle and the calves that needed branding. It was the time the big outfits would be out, too, she said, leaving unsaid the other thing: that she had to see that her interests were protected against the big ranches, no matter what business these two outsiders had with each other.

"And when they're gone," she said sternly, squinting at him as he rested in the sun beside the door to her house, "I'll think about giving your guns back to you."

Alvarez gave her his best toothy smile. "You know, Miz Diemert, there'll be trouble between us when he comes back—if he comes back." It should have been a time to play his cards close to the vest, and with another adversary he might have, but his instincts told him that bold forthrightness was the best plan now. Alvarez always went with his instincts. Anyway, this woman wasn't stupid; she must have already thought just what he was telling her.

"Perhaps, Marshal. But he's proved to be a good man so far. A hard worker, and God-fearing."

"I still have to arrest him if I can."

Her eyes clouded, and he could see in them that some great decision had been reached, that the Bible reading and praying had brought her to some conclusion that she would not share aloud with him, at least not for now.

But he had won.

"You do what you think is just, Marshal," she said. "So long as you understand . . . he's proved to be a good worker and a kind man." And then she left him to sit there alone in the sunshine.

It was that very evening, while Joe was packing his things for the roundup and telling his sisters that this was the sort of adventure that would make him a man, that Tom Alvarez watched Billy Shingleton and Cora Diemert talking in the shadows near the shed. They didn't see Alvarez, for he was in shadow alongside the house himself, and they were too far away to hear the thudding of his crutches against the earth.

He watched them and tried without success to hear what they were saying. They were talking earnestly, and whatever she was saying angered Shingleton at first, but when he tried to break away she held out her hands and took him by the arms to soothe him. When he tried to pull away again, this time without any spirit, she held him. As a lover might.

Then, for a brief moment, there had been silence between them, and Cora Diemert had looked away. Billy Shingleton's hands came up to her face slowly, gently, and he bent down and kissed her on the cheek. Before she could react, he turned and strode away into the purple evening, past the cottonwood and onto the open plain.

CHAPTER 12

FRANK McAlester lay on his stomach in the short grass of the mesa. Below, the summer heat had set the world to shimmering, distorting his view of the wide, V-shaped plateau wedged in between the chop hills and the arroyos. From this distance, he could see the cottonwood and the house and the outbuildings, but very little else. There was someone moving in the yard, but whether it was a man or a woman, he couldn't be sure. He wished he had his good binoculars, especially now that the passing years had robbed him of the sharpness of his sun-bleached eyes. But the glasses were gone, lost to pay off a five dollar debt in a poker game down in Fort Stanton two summers back. They'd never been missed until now.

He watched for a while longer, then slid on his stomach Indian-fashion until he was back from the lip of the mesa. No telling whether someone down there had good eyesight without field glasses! Only when he was well back of the edge did he rise and trot down the cut on the far side to where his horse stood hobbled and content to browse the heat-ripened grass.

Their camp was three miles away along a little dry streambed that fed into the Canadian. He wished he'd been able to send Rawley Thomas on this scout. It would have done the boy good to learn a little patience, but he wasn't ready yet. If he'd taken the turn-down better when he asked to go along, McAlester might have relented, but the black grumbling moodiness had sealed it: Rawley was staying put. Frank McAlester was paid to know his men and use them the best way he could. He prided himself on that. And Rawley, for all his good points, was so impatient that he'd ruin their plans if given half a chance. An impatient man could get himself and his friends into a lot of trouble. They couldn't afford that. Not until they were ready.

He kicked his horse in the slats and they loped off for the camp.

They'd all agreed not to just ride onto the woman's place the way they had before, when that kid had surprised them and come near to dry-gulching Rawley. They simply couldn't take that kind of chance again. Not if the kid was still there. And even if he wasn't, a little surprise, a little strategy would work better to dislodge the woman from her place than sheer brute force. That had been the plan, at least, before his reconnoiter.

But something else was going on.

Damn, but he did wish he'd been able to keep those field glasses. Even though he could tell that something was wrong at the woman's place, he couldn't get a good enough look to tell what.

It wasn't so much that he'd seen it as that he'd felt it in his bones, smelled it in the wind along with summer dust and burnt saltbush. Well, careful planning might take care of that, whatever it was. And in the meantime, there was work to do.

The cowboys didn't rise when he rode in as they would have for John Chisum or Rudy Miller, but they did lift their hats from their eyes and prop themselves up on their elbows where they'd sprawled in the shade of the cook's wagon. The small, fierce fires of morning that had been used to heat the branding irons were burned to ashes now, and the makeshift corrals they'd thrown up to hold the unbranded calves were empty, their contents sent bawling over the prairie. The market-ready yearlings had already been moved to the little box canyon where a couple of the boys could hold them until it was time to head them south toward the railhead. The air still smelled of burnt hair and hide and man-sweat, and the dust of the campsite had been stirred and broken and kicked up until there was a fine yellow film of it on everything.

McAlester tied his mount to the picket line and slumped down in the shade. The cook offered him a cup of thick, bitter coffee, boiling hot in the tin cup. He took it, juggling it gingerly and blowing on it to cool it some before he gulped it down. The cowboys watched him silently, and even Rawley waited for him to stretch out and finish the coffee. These men didn't talk much, but then they weren't paid for talking. McAlester liked them, as a teacher likes a classroom full of spirited pupils eager to learn.

"I got to figure on this one a while, boys," he said at last.

Rawley's face darkened, and McAlester saw the muscles of his jaw tighten. Still, Rawley didn't get up from his place in the shade. That was a good sign, McAlester reckoned. Control.

"We got the firepower, boss," one of the younger kids said, and as if to prove his point, he hauled a Colt's .45 out of the waistband of his baggy trousers.

McAlester only hawked phlegm and spit it into the dust and pretended to ignore the kid.

"Whyn't we just shoot hell outen 'em?" the kid asked, and he pointed his piece at a clump of saltbush just outside the camp circle as if he were drawing down on a human target.

"Put that thing away," McAlester said slowly. "And get you a decent holster. You go riding after steers with that damn cannon tucked in your britches, you'll apt to blow your nuts off and kill a good cow pony in the process. I doubt the boss would mind you turnin' yourself into a steer, but a good horse is hard to find."

The other boys laughed, and the offender blushed bright red through the grime and leather-deep tan.

McAlester looked over his shoulder for the cook.

"Swisher! You still got the holster for that six-shooter you lost crossing the Pecos last spring?"

"I do," the cook answered sourly, and all the boys stirred in anticipation of what was coming next. McAlester had ridden the cook unmercifully about losing that gun until the old man—at forty-some, the oldest in the trail outfit by better than a dozen years except for McAlester himself—had threatened to up and quit. Even now, the foreman would tease him over it whenever he got too bossy or his biscuits got too dry.

"Well, then, why don't you give it to Pete, since he's got himself a forty-five and no place to carry it except inside his union suit."

"Cost him a buck," the cook grumbled. There was resignation more than real anger in his voice; he knew he'd already lost the holster, but it didn't pay to give anything up without getting even-or-better in return.

"Hell, boss, I ain't got any cash money at all," Pete protested.

"Fifty cents, then," McAlester said, obviously enjoying the banter. "On credit, to be paid at the end of the roundup."

"I won't take a cent less than six bits," the cook said testily.

"But I ain't got it!"

"Six bits and sold!" McAlester shouted. "And it's a hell of a buy at the price, Pete, though I reckon it's a mite shrunk from too much time in the water. Ain't that true, Swish?"

"Shit," the cook said. He went behind the wagon to rummage around in his personal gear. When he came up with the holster, he tossed it to Pete. "I kept that thing oiled so it'd be as soft as a whore's butt. You keep it that way, hear, or I'll take it back. And you owe me six bits, soon as we hit the ranch."

McAlester laughed again and ordered more coffee. It would be an hour before supper, and there was time to rest a little since it was Sunday. Most trail bosses worked the boys dawn to dark every day during the roundup, but McAlester had learned a long time ago that men, like horses, need a breather once in a while to get their second wind, to keep from fagging out altogether. Give them half of Sunday afternoon to sit in the shade or play the mouth organ or read a little from the sack of dog-eared books he managed to smuggle onto the cook's wagon or even say their prayers if they were of a mind, and they'd be good for another week of backbreaking work afoot and on horseback.

The books were important to Frank McAlester. He'd have brought them along even if Rudy Miller hadn't approved, just as he'd brought books onto the trail back when old John Chisum was active and raving that any cowboy of his who had the time to read was damned sure not earning his pay. McAlester did his best thinking when he was reading, with his eyes skimming the pages and his conscious mind absorbing the Shakespeare or Fenimore Cooper or Hawthorne. It was at those times that somewhere, in the back of his mind where he wasn't even aware of it, the good thoughts and plans would come together. Whenever a problem really had him stumped, he went to the chuckwagon and got himself a book to read.

As soon as he finished off the second cup of coffee, he got up and found *Moby Dick* and sat down again with Ishmael and Starbuck and Ahab on the rolling seas. Maybe little Pete was right. Maybe the thing to do was to go in shooting and get them off the place once and for all.

But maybe there was a better way, too.

He opened the book and started to read.

They broke camp the next morning. Little groups of riders looking for more strays to herd toward the branding corrals fanned out to the north and east. McAlester stayed behind with the cook. The boys would be out for two days, maybe three. On Thursday, they'd finish branding what needed branding, then move the whole camp ten or fifteen miles north to hunt new pasturage.

McAlester let Swisher take a little nap after the boys rode out. The cook had been up most of the night fixing a good hot breakfast of steak, oatmeal, and corn bread—the last good feed the boys would have until they came rolling in on Tuesday night or Wednesday trailing the yearlings and spring calves. In the meantime, they'd have to live off boiled beans and biscuits Swisher had packed into their saddlebags.

When the cook awakened, the two men sat in the shade of the wagon and played poker for a few hours. It was nearly noon before McAlester let Swisher win the final hand and then saddled up his horse to ride back to the little mesa where he'd spied on the woman. He didn't want to go back, but he needed more information. She wouldn't shoot a lone rider, he supposed, and neither would the young man with her. At least that was the way he was betting.

Maybe he could use reason one more time, try just once more to appeal to her to see it the way it had to be.

And if that didn't work . . .

Well, Pete was right. They had the guns. Rawley was clearly itching to use his. If it came to that, one more reconnoiter of the place wouldn't hurt a bit.

"You take it easy, Swish," McAlester said as he mounted, but the cook was not paying attention, and after a moment he heard why.

Gunfire, faint as the rustle of leaves, but gunfire nonetheless. A distance away, to the north.

McAlester sat stock still on his horse, his eyes straining against the white light of midday. When he saw the thin wisp of black smoke rising straight into the air along the horizon, he nudged the horse into a lope in that direction. It was smoke that came from no branding fire.

CHAPTER 13

HOEING the garden had become brutally hard for her. The spongy softness of the ground the first few days after the cloudburst had disappeared as the summer sun sucked the moisture from the soil, leaving flint-hard clay in its wake. The only reminder of the rain that was still left was the crazy-quilt pattern of cracks in the soil where the mud had dried and split, the edges curling so a person could lift out a flat wafer of earth that seemed to hold together out of sheer stubbornness until the slightest tap crumbled it into nothing but dust.

Her son would have been a big help in the garden, but hoeing was too much for the girls. Joe was in one of those growth spurts that amazed her; he seemed to be gaining strength every day, regardless of the poor diet of salt pork and corn bread. It was more important that he help with the roundup.

So the tough August weeds had to be chopped out with a sharpened hoe, and even that was only a temporary salvation; a beheaded thistle would grow back sturdier than ever in a few days, and on the edges of the garden, the tumbleweeds were already drying, readying themselves for the autumn winds that would carry them across the plains. The weeds thrived in the brick-hard soil, as if they had some magical claim on whatever moisture and nutrients were there, leaving nothing for the crops. Her corn was browning along the edges of the leaves, the ears drooping not with the heaviness of fat sweet kernels, but with fatigue and starvation. The dust worked away from the bases of the stalks, and the exposed roots barely kept the plants upright. The peppers and squash were doing some better, but the other truck she'd planted, the potatoes and yams and onions, were pitiful things that a smart farmer would have plowed under. Still, she refused to give up on them, and so she hoed and sweated and hoped.

Of course, they'd need more luck than Cora Diemert had any right to expect. A ten-year-old boy and a Kansas bank robber barely twice that age didn't stand much chance of finding and branding more than a handful of Diemert cattle—maybe not that many, depending on how much of the herd was left. She could not forget Joe's story of seeing the carcass buried in the sand after the flood.

And then there was Billy Shingleton.

She pushed the sunbonnet back on her head to keep it from falling into her eyes as she worked. She chopped fiercely at a goathead, the low burr that grew everywhere in this New Mexico wilderness.

Even now, her cheek still burned from his brushing kiss, as if his lips had been hot coals. Or perhaps what burned inside her was shame, the revulsion over having allowed such a thing to happen. Guilt, mingled with the other feelings she could not wish away. She had bottled those feelings up until the moment when he had stood over her and she had allowed the anguish to well up into her eyes, where he could see it.

She had longed for that brushing kiss, but she had feared it, too. And now that it was over, she longed for another. There was her shame, as ugly and unyielding as the goatheads and thistles she attacked with the hoe.

Cora Diemert stood up to straighten and to rest her aching back, and as she did so, she found herself facing the cottonwood tree. Its shadow was only beginning the march across the yard toward her, but as the afternoon progressed, it would come for her, the individual shadows of its branches like the tentacles of some fabled sea monster, groping for her. She imagined Henry sitting there at the base of the tree as he had in their first days on this place, reading his seed catalogues.

It was the cottonwood that had attracted him to this piece of ground from the first, had convinced him that this was where they must put down their roots after the long heartache-filled journey from their first home. She remembered with absolute clarity how it was with him when they'd spotted the tree standing alone in this little swale.

The tree proved there was water near the surface, Henry had said, and his eyes had gleamed with the thought. Even before Cora had finished with the supper she'd fixed over an open fire built where the house now stood, he'd begun to dig his well. She shaded her eyes and looked into the sun. The windmill creaked obligingly; if she really listened, she could hear the trickle of water pouring into the tank.

They'd worked themselves half to death those first few weeks, what with hauling water from the river, cutting sod and baking the 'dobe for the house, and taking the wagon into Wagon Mound twice for lumber, nails, and what other supplies they could afford. Meanwhile, Henry had kept to his digging in every spare moment. The sand under the sod was damp, but no water pooled in the hole at night; after two weeks he'd hitched up the team again and ridden all the way to Springer to talk to the banker about a loan.

Loan money would buy a seed herd and pay for the equipment to sink a decent well where a windmill could do the work. It would buy a new buckboard to replace their worn-out old wagon, and it would buy an iron stove and the bobwire to fence off the livestock and to keep the roaming herds of the big ranches off the place.

Cora hadn't understood at first why the banker had been so ready to lend them his money, but now she knew. There had never been any hope that Henry Diemert could pay off the debt: the banker's hospitality had been a sham with an eye toward that day when foreclosure was a certainty. Let them improve the place, buy the cattle, dig the well, and then the bank would take it all from them for unpaid interest. The bank would claim the herd and the land once they started missing their payments. More importantly, it would then control the access to the land—access that would bring a pretty penny from the ranchers like Rudy Miller. It was a simple-enough scheme and one that she'd seen through after a time. She'd argued with Henry about it, but he couldn't or wouldn't believe it. If he'd lived, they'd have lost the place already.

But Cora Diemert wasn't moving. At least not because the cowboys harassed her or the banker came to threaten foreclosure.

Nothing was moving her off this place until she was ready.

She didn't love the land. Not like Henry had. The only land she'd ever loved was back home in Missouri, at the home place and in the little graveyard where she'd buried her boy.

No, she wouldn't fight for the land itself, but she *would* fight for the right to be where she wished, the right to raise her children wherever she chose without being beholden to anyone. She'd leave in her own time and in her own way, and not before.

Except that now there were these other complications.

Billy Shingleton was one of them, and so was Marshal Tom Alvarez. Billy had come as an answer to her prayers, the avenging angel who might help her hold the land against the cowboys in spite of the loss of her man, only now it turned out that he was a robber and a killer, just the kind of dangerous cutthroat she'd expected to find in this inhospitable place from the very first. She hated Tom Alvarez for telling her about Billy, though she knew it was his duty. Now she had to stand between this boy and the man who hunted him—a hard, determined man she did not like but who nonetheless represented law and order and decency and all those civilized things Cora Diemert deeply believed in.

She rubbed her hands across her forehead and turned her eyes away from the cottonwood. In two weeks, she would be thirty-four years old, yet she felt a hundred. Her hands had grown big-knuckled from years with hoe and washboard, her palms shiny with old calluses. Squinting into the sun had set deep wrinkles in the corners of her eyes, and her chestnut hair was faded from sun and hard times, and now it was streaked with gray. She was almost thirty-four years old, and for a long time she had believed that the quickening of the heart, the soft flushing of the face that a man had once caused in her were things gone forever, as the sweet innocence of her youth was gone.

Now there was Billy Shingleton.

Chop went the hoe as she swung it after a goathead.

No matter how hard she tried to keep from thinking of him, she could not.

A cutthroat. A gentle boy, a hard worker. Underneath the tough shell, a sentimental man with a kind heart.

A lump came to her throat and she fought back the tears, rubbing at her eyes with the back of her hand.

Chop.

She didn't know that Tom Alvarez had come to watch.

He stood in the little sliver of shade beside the house for a long time. It was his favorite place now, since he had discovered that he could command a view of the entire yard without being seen. He leaned easily against the house as he watched.

He couldn't help but admire her. She was working terribly hard. This woman was a strong one for the frontier, one of the few who would survive despite what man and nature would throw at her. He'd seen many women crack under the hardships of the Kansas plains, and Kansas had been civilized far longer than this corner of New Mexico where scarcely a dozen years ago the Kiowas and Comanches had hunted buffalo and no white man had dared to come. Now it was cow country.

That, of course, was her problem. She would survive, but

not on her own terms. This *was* cattle country, with ripe grass and plenty of open country; what had served the buffalo would now serve the ranchers who could control hundreds of thousands of acres of free land. But Cora Diemert wasn't equipped to run a cattle operation. He'd overheard her talking about it enough to know that her herd was too small to compete with those of the big ranchers. She had only two boys out trying to carry out a full-fledged roundup! It was only a matter of time before she would lose the place. Maybe grasshoppers or another cloudburst or a blizzard would finish her off quickly. If some natural disaster didn't, then the terrible economies of running a small place in a large country would whittle her away until there was nothing left.

The day would come when Cora Diemert would be a dried-out husk, ready to blow away in the first strong wind like the tumbleweeds she was attacking in the garden.

It was surely a pity.

On the spur of the moment, he left his spying-place in the shade and hobbled toward her, leaning heavily on his crutch as he went. The leg was feeling better now; he fancied that he'd be able to ride before long. Still, it would be many years before it was as strong as it once had been, and it would always be a little crooked.

She stood up and stretched the ache out of her back when he came into the garden, but she did not speak.

"Mrs. Diemert," he said, nodding. "You're working too hard on such a hot day."

She shielded her eyes with her hand and glared at him.

"I'd be obliged," he said, "if you'd let me do a little of the weeding. It would be good for me to do some work around here."

"Your leg won't stand it."

"I can use the crutch. It'll have to stand it sooner or later."

She shrugged and handed him the hoe. From the way she stepped back and crossed her arms over the front of her dusty dress, it was plain that she didn't think he'd be able to work for very long before the leg gave out. She would just stand and wait for that to happen.

He smiled and took the hoe in his strong right hand while he used the left to brace his weight against the crutch. He took a couple of practice swings to be sure of his balance and then, using the hoe the way he would a scythe, swung again in earnest. The strength came into his arm slowly; he had been inactive for too long. Even so, it felt good to use his muscles again, to feel the slight burning sensation of over-exertion, to be aware of the sharper pumping of his heart and the heat the moving blood carried throughout his body. His leg hurt, and so did his left arm from fighting for balance against the heavy swinging movements of his right side, but it was a good hurt that told him he was alive and strong still.

"I haven't worked like this in a long time," he said without looking up from his hoeing. "Not since I was a kid, maybe."

She said nothing.

"I grew up in Missouri," he said. "Same as you. I can tell from your voice. Ozarks?"

"Yes," she said curtly, as if she didn't want to discuss it.

"My people settled up around Jefferson City. We were from Pennsylvania, but we moved west before the war. My dad had been a cobbler in the East, but we farmed in Missouri. Hogs." He paused to catch his breath. This was tough work on one good leg. "Hogs! When I was your boy's age, I was scared to death I was going to waste the rest of my life raising pigs. Maybe that's why I went to lawing. For the pure excitement of it." He laughed easily at the memory.

"We lived down in the hills in Douglas County. Goodhope was the nearest town," she said.

He stopped to move down the row a little and to mop his brow.

She was still standing there with her arms folded. He thought he saw a trace of grudging admiration in the look she gave him.

He finished the row and started another.

"Please don't overdo, Marshal," she said at last.

He paused again to catch his breath. "Mrs. Diemert, a man needs to use his body. I've been lying around for too long. If I stay much longer, I'll be as soft as an old feather pillow." He laughed, and she joined him with a laugh of her own that was both soft and genuine.

"Well, we certainly can't have that, can we?"

He grinned. "No, ma'am. I've got work ahead of me that I need to be ready for."

He saw the dark shadow cross her face and he wished he had not said it. She was angry with him again, both for allowing herself the weakness of such pleasantries and because he represented such a vast complication of her life.

"You may not believe it," he said, "but I take no pleasure in what I have to do with Billy Shingleton. It's my job. What the government pays me to do. And I'm good at it. I take pride in it. But I take no pleasure."

Once again, she was silent.

He went back to chopping a particularly tough weed. Something else was nagging at him, something he knew needed saying, and he knew there might never be a better time. "I want to thank you, too, for what you've done for me. I didn't expect to find such kindness out here. Or such courage, for that matter. You're truly a courageous woman, Mrs. Diemert." The words embarrassed him because he knew they would embarrass her.

"You work as long as you wish," she said quickly, and then she stumped into the house, leaving him alone in the hot sun.

Her hands shook as she prepared the noon meal of cold corn bread and the last of the canned peaches Henry had bought in Wagon Mound. She'd butchered a chicken for their supper and it was already in the stewing pot on the stove. She'd hoped the hot work would get her mind off what it was that troubled her, but she hadn't succeeded. Instead, she'd burned herself twice while singeing the chicken, and her hands were so unsteady that she could hardly move the heavy pot around the stove without spilling it.

Cora felt as if some part of her were drowning, as if she were losing contact with the real world around her.

Damn Billy Shingleton, she said under her breath, then immediately she said a prayer asking forgiveness for the oath. But anyway: damn Billy Shingleton and Tom Alvarez into the bargain, too. No one had asked these men to come to her place and upset her life. Weren't things complicated enough? Wasn't it bad enough that she had to try to hold the place together against the bankers and ranchers without Henry? As God himself could judge, she had been doing a poor job of raising the children even before these men had come. Joe, who should be coming on to manhood, kept to himself too much and watched and listened too much when he should have been working, thinking, helping. And the girls were like wild Indians, growing up together, looking after each other with precious little guidance from a mother who was too busy to care for them properly.

They needed a firm hand, those girls. And Joe needed the example only a strong father could give him. Instead, they had only her, and she was stretched too thin, kept too busy just keeping them all alive to give them the guidance they needed. She feared that if they managed to hold onto this Godforsaken piece of dirt long enough to make it pay, to own it free and clear, her children would be ruined for all time, the last remnants of the gentility of their people back in Missouri erased from them as surely as the roaring floods back home had erased the stubble and furrows of the bottomland fields. And if they could not hold on, if they lost this place, then there would be the mark of Cain upon them, too—the black mark of failure. Joe had already seen what failure could do to a man; the time would come soon enough when he'd be looking, as his father's son, for that weakness in himself.

So there was her dilemma. To hold on here meant that she must abandon her children to the harsh realities, the wild uncivilized nature of this place. To admit defeat would be to renounce their heritage as Diemerts and Galts, the good people who were their forebears.

So didn't she have enough troubles without Tom Alvarez and Billy Shingleton? What trick of fate had brought them riding here in the first place? And what crueller trick had kept them?

And why, just now, did the thought of their leaving fill her with some strange new dread? Was it because the day they left would inevitably be the day that Tom Alvarez would be taking Billy Singleton back to Kansas to hang?

Unbidden, the other, darker thought intruded on her: that Billy would kill Alvarez and thus escape his punishment on earth, if not in heaven.

Billy . . .

Her hands shook so that she had to sit down for a moment and clasp them tightly in her lap. The trembling ran up her arms and her whole body shook as if from a chill. Then it passed, but she recognized it for exactly what it was.

Shame. And a deep caring that she had not felt for years, since the first days when she and Henry had been together, when the whole world had looked young and green and full of promise.

The door opened and Tom Alvarez stepped inside. Perspiration was streaming down his face, and his clothes were gray from garden dust.

"You should wash, sir, before coming . . ."

He held up his strong right hand to silence her.

"Mrs. Diemert, please tell me where my guns are."

"No."

"Something has happened and I need to be armed."

"What . . . what's happened?"

"I don't know, but something." He turned and stepped outside, stopping only to beckon her to follow.

She rose and went into the yard with him. As soon as she turned the corner of the house, she saw the pall of black smoke hanging along the northern horizon.

CHAPTER 14

THE boy gathered up the cooled branding irons and wrestled them into the big burlap sack he kept secured with one of his father's old belts. Every bone in his body felt bruised and every muscle ached. He could not remember ever being more tired, but it was important that he not show it, at least not now. Bill Smith was stretched out in the shade under the wagon to catch a few winks before he put the coffee and bacon on the fire. After the usual greasy lunch, they'd move on, looking for more cows and calves. Bill had told him how well he was doing, how like a man he was, and so now was the time to prove it, to stay alert and keep working even when his body was crying out for rest.

The days had been long for them, and in his heart, Joe was glad that they'd only found a few ragged bunches of Diemert cattle to work. Bill had had plenty of trouble with the culling and cutting, especially since Alvarez's big horse hadn't been bred for the work of a cow pony; and they'd seen as many yearlings and calves bolt up the arroyos and disappear back into the scrub oak and saltbush as they'd seen secure on the end of a pigging string for branding. Even with their herd small and scattered, they could have used four or five trained cowboys for this work, and neither Bill Smith nor Joe Diemert qualified.

Still, it *was* exciting work. They didn't talk much except for what the work demanded, which only made Joe feel bigger and more important. Once, on a slow afternoon, they'd given up work for a little target shooting, but even that hadn't equalled the thrill of the roundup. The soreness and dirt and noise and the smells of hot iron and burnt hide and horse sweat were all etched into Joe's memory; this was something he would never forget.

Joe heaved the burlap bundle onto the wagon and mopped the sweat out of his eyes with his grime-caked shirt sleeve. That was when he saw them, all standing abreast on a little ridge five or six hundred yards away. There were ten of them, just sitting there, and he knew right away who they were.

His knees turned to rubber beneath him.

"Bill," he said as clearly as his voice would allow, "we got visitors. Cowboys." Then he took a deep breath to calm himself and reached into the buggy to extract the big handgun that belonged to Tom Alvarez.

Bill sat up and peered in the direction that Joe indicated.

"I'll say we got company!" he said.

He scrambled out from under the wagon and retrieved his own weapon. He slipped it into the waistband of his trousers, but loosely enough that he could draw it easily. Only then did he sweep off his hat and wave it high above his head, as if to signal the riders.

They waited a moment, then spurred their mounts into an easy canter down the ridge. They reined in at a hundred yards, still all ten abreast.

"I got the marshal's gun, Bill," Joe said as calmly as he knew how. "I can use it."

Bill spat into the dust and absently scuffed over the wet spot with the toe of his boot. "Not at this range, boy. Besides, you ain't never shot at anything that was alive. Why don't you just lay that gun down calm as all hell, and maybe there won't be no trouble. Could be a social call."

"I recognize 'em, Bill. I seen 'em before. At the house."

Bill laughed a low, easy chuckle. "I know, boy. Me too. But do me a favor and put the gun down anyhow. I don't want you hurt." Then he shuffled sideways, away from the wagon and out into the open and away from the boy. He waved his hat again, but with his left hand so the right would stay free.

"You men want some coffee?" he hollered at the top of his lungs. The wind was with him, and he knew that they heard him, but they cupped their hands to their ears as if they didn't understand.

He waved once more and then deliberately turned his back on them and walked slowly to the fire. He picked up the coffee pot and settled it in among the glowing embers. He knelt carefully and poked a stick at the coals to bring them back to life. It was a good fire, with plenty of heat still in it; in a few minutes, the pot would be singing.

"They comin'?" he asked without turning around.

"Yes," Joe answered.

This time, the cowboys came all the way, and this time they broke ranks to surround the little camp. Joe felt his heart pounding, and he knew that the fear showed on his face, but he couldn't help it. Bill, on the other hand, was as cool as if these were old friends dropping by for a visit. He'd slipped on his work gloves so he could handle the coffee pot, and he rose to extend the gloved hand to the visitors. He had a smile on his face—a mocking, calculating smile that scared Joe almost as much as the cowboys did.

"You two doin' some brandin'?" one of the cowboys asked.

"Sure. Diemert calves," Bill answered. He cocked his head toward the one who had spoken. "Don't I know you? Believe I seen you at the Diemert place once."

The cowboy ignored the question. "Found some Miller stock with a strange brand yesterday. What brand you usin'?"

"Bar-Cross-D. Like an 'H' and a 'D' run together. Registered over to Wagon Mound."

"Ought to register in Fort Stanton or Santa Rosa." The cowboy leader looked at one of the others with him. That what you seen, Gus? A Bar-Cross-D?"

The one spoken to just nodded.

"Couldn't of been Miller stock, then," Bill said evenly. Joe saw that he now had his right hand resting easily on the butt of the revolver in his trousers. "We've been real careful to mark only calves and yearlings running with other Bar-Cross-D cows. And to be honest, we haven't found too many of them, neither."

"Yeh, it's just him and me working alone," Joe said quickly, surprising himself. In the same instant, he saw the tightness in Bill's jaw and the half-smile that came over the lead cowboy's face. He opened his mouth again as he tried to think of a way out, but none came. He had said something best left unmentioned.

"Just two of you, huh?" the cowboy said.

"That's right, Rawley," Bill said slowly, and he deliberately moved a little closer to the dying fire. "Your name is Rawley, ain't it?"

The cowboy's smile faded. "Could be. Don't reckon I caught yours."

"Bill. Bill Shingleton."

"Well, we found Rudy Miller's calves running with your brand. And they was following Miller cows. Reckon you owe us somewheres around fifty, sixty head."

"Hell, we ain't branded that many, total."

"Don't call me a liar, boy."

"Don't believe I am," Bill said coolly. "Just tellin' the truth."

"Then how you goin' to pay for fifty head of beeves?"

"I ain't."

"The hell you ain't."

The faint trace of a smile returned to Bill's face. "The hell I am." He took two steps backward without taking his eyes off the cowboys and swung his leg in an arc through the center of the little fire. His foot caught the coffee pot square, sending it clattering onto the ground and scattering red-hot coals with it. Upended, the pot splattered scalding coffee onto the legs of one of the cowboys' horses; the animal reared and bucked once, and the rider swore out loud. Quirting the animal around the ears, the cowboy wrestled it to a standstill. The horse snorted but didn't buck again.

Joe, who had been watching the horse, looked back toward

the one called Rawley now and saw that he hadn't been distracted by Bill's kick. Bill had moved for his own gun while the horse danced, but Rawley had been a half second faster: his big .44 was out and aimed easily across his saddle horn at Bill's heart.

"Cute, mister," Rawley said. "Now we got some tradin' to do."

All the cowboys drew their guns, and in what seemed to Joe like the next heartbeat, all hell broke loose.

He dived under the wagon and squirmed around to watch. The cowboys were shooting wildly and whooping and cursing, emptying their .44s into the air or the ground as fast as they could pull the triggers. Their horses stamped and rolled their eyes at the noise and smoke.

Tom Alvarez's big horse jerked free of its picket stake and thundered through the center of the camp and between two of the smaller cow ponies. Joe could see one of the cowboys take two quick shots at the fleeing horse, but the bullets went wide. The mule wasn't so lucky. It set up a loud braying over the racket of the shooting, then went suddenly quiet. Joe rolled over to get a look at it and saw it totter and fall all splay-legged, the frothy blood pouring from its nostrils, its tongue hanging out of its mouth.

He looked for Bill and found him still standing by the fire, his hands high in the air. Then the wagon above Joe began to rock. One wheel rose clear off the ground and came down with a thud beside his head. Panic rose up and overwhelmed him; he scooted out from under the wagon and ran toward Bill.

One of the cowboys spurred his mount and caught the running boy by the suspenders and lifted him clear of the ground. Man and boy and horse swung wide of the rest of the group.

Joe heard rather than saw the wagon fall over on its side, to the louder whooping of the cowboys. Then another horse bolted past, this time with a rider trailing a lariat. Bill Smith was at the end of the rope, half running and half being dragged behind the galloping pony.

The cowboy holding Joe in the air let out a yell and dropped the boy.

Joe hit the ground hard, face-first, and rolled head over heels. Hooves pounded all around him, kicking up a choking cloud of dust. One horse reared, and both front feet came down within inches of his face. He tried to sit up, but all the blood drained out of his head. Great black dots swam in his eyes, and he slid out of consciousness.

We awoke with a jolt. Bill was sitting beside him. Joe struggled to make his eyes focus on his friend. Both Bill's eyes were blackened, his nose pushed over to the side, broken, his clothing tattered and smeared with brown drying blood. As Joe watched, Bill seemed to disappear in a gray haze.

Joe smelled smoke and it dawned on him that drifting ashes were settling over both of them. He turned a little and saw that the wagon was nothing but a pile of cinders. Only one wheel and the metal parts were still recognizable, and all their gear lay strewn out on the ground, smoldering.

The cowboy called Rawley rode his horse up to them and leaned over as far as he could so he could look Bill directly in his puffy eyes.

"We ought to of killed you for stealin' Miller cattle, mister. We didn't, but we ought to've. Next time, you won't be so damn lucky. You tell your woman that, hear?" Grinning, he uncoiled a length of rope and whipped Bill across the face, opening a gash across his cheek.

Rawley let out a rebel yell and dug his knees into his horse's flanks. It bolted straight over them and through the campsite past the burning wagon and out onto the plain. The other cowboys followed, and the last Bill and Joe saw of them, they were riding jauntily over the ridge, all ten once again abreast.

Bill struggled to his feet and wiped at the blood on his face. He bent over suddenly and heaved, but nothing came up. He heaved a second time and spit and wiped at his lips with a torn sleeve.

"You all right, Joe?" he asked at last.

"Yessir. I think." Joe moved his arms and legs to make sure nothing was broken. He had a terrific headache, but that was all.

"Good."

"You're an awful mess."

"Well, maybe. But not so awful as that bastard will be the next time I see him." Bill worked at the broken nose to straighten it, and Joe could hear the torn cartilage grating. A clot broke free, and for a few seconds the nose bled freely, but Bill pushed a gloved finger against his upper lip, and in a moment the flow stopped.

Joe sat up slowly. Once again, the black dots swam, but this time he managed to keep his wits about him. He fought against the dizziness and conquered it. "Why'd they do it? Why'd they do it, Bill?"

"Just bastards, that's all. Want to push you and your momma off the range."

"But why?"

Joe rubbed at his stinging eyes and took a good, long look at the burned-out wagon and the carcass of the mule. This, too, was a sight he knew he'd never forget—and, in a strange way, would never want to forget. He was just ten years old, but for the first time in his life, he knew hatred. "The bastards!" he said aloud, and the saying of the forbidden words felt strong in his heart.

"You up to helping me track down that big horse of the marshal's? I figure we best get back to your momma quick."

Joe looked at him. "Sure."

Bill sifted through the remnants of their gear until he found Alvarez's revolver, and then together they began the long walk in search of Tom Alvarez's horse.

CHAPTER 15

CORA and Alvarez were still watching the column of black smoke on the northern horizon curl lazily upward and fan out on the soft breeze when Frank McAlester rode into the yard alone. They had not even heard his coming, so intent had they been on watching the smoke.

Later, thinking back on the confrontation between the woman and the cowboy, it occurred to Alvarez that a man in Cora's place would have been consumed with blazing anger at the rider's taunts and intimidation—and that anger would have played right into the rider's hands. But Cora was an exceptional woman. She stood her ground and took the verbal abuse without so much as a blink.

Until the final moment, when the cowboy leaned far over his saddle toward her and, in a voice Alvarez could barely hear, threatened the lives of her children.

That threat had been there all along, but until that moment it had remained unsaid. Once the words were spoken aloud, the thin veneer of control that had been her strength crumbled; both the cowboy and Alvarez saw the twitching muscles in her face and the trembling in her hands. Suddenly, her nerves were strained beyond the breaking point. The cowboy had won something very important; he grinned and tipped his hat to her, then put spurs to his horse and galloped off her place.

Alvarez watched Cora as the cowboy rode off.

"I wish I could have helped," he said, and it was true. It had been a long time since he had felt helpless in the face of danger, but he did now. "If you'd let me have my guns . . ."

But she wasn't listening. She turned and went into the house alone.

The hot afternoon faded into warm evening and still she and the children stayed inside. Alvarez puttered around the yard, brought as much firewood to the door as he could handle on crutches, and put down some cracked corn for chickens. As the last trace of red was fading from the sky, he knocked softly on the door and opened it.

The only light came from around the firebox on the stove, and he could smell coffee. That was a good sign.

"I'd surely love a cup of coffee," he said. "I've worked a sight harder that I should with this leg." He closed the door behind him and sank into a chair at the table.

Cora's hands were still shaking as she poured the coffee for him. Her girls, sensing their mother's fear, sat quietly on their bed peering into the gloom.

Alvarez smiled at them, and they looked away in shyness. He sipped his coffee and let time pass.

"Do you think it's an idle threat?" she asked the marshal, breaking the silence only after his first cup of coffee was gone and she had poured another. "Can they burn us out?"

"They can and they will," he said quietly, without reminding her that they still didn't know what had caused the smoke they had seen at midday.

"Are you sure?"

It was time to say what he had been thinking, but there was no need to rush into it.

"I admire you for your coolness," he said. "It's a fine thing to stand your ground like that, no matter what. But you heard a genuine threat this afternoon. He meant business. And there's a fine line between being brave and being foolhardy."

"We're here by rights," she said. "This is free land, here for the taking. We have a claim."

"Claims don't mean a thing to them."

"You're the law, aren't you? The law ought to stop them."

"Not until after they've done the deed. By then it may be too late for you." He opened his mouth to ask her again for his guns, but changed his mind.

"His threat isn't against the law?"

"Maybe, but at most it's be between you and the cowboys and some local constable. I haven't seen any constables around here I'd trust, especially in Wagon Mound. I might have been able to help today, but . . ."

"But I wouldn't let you." Her voice was flat and matter-of-fact.

He nodded and sipped the coffee.

She brushed a wisp of hair out of her face. "Then what do I do now?"

He looked at her in the darkness and tried to make out her features. The voice wasn't pleading yet; she wasn't a beggar. Her question sought advice, but nothing more. She had two helpless daughters, a son away on a ridiculous roundup she hoped would hold this place together while she faced a serious threat, and yet even now she clearly was weighing her options. As if she had any.

"Mrs. Diemert, my advice is to pack up and move away from here. Give them the range. They'll take it one way or another anyway. Take your kids somewhere else, where they can have a life."

"That's your advice." It wasn't a question.

"That's it."

She rose and went to the stove to fiddle with the coffee again. There was a certain firmness about her now that hadn't been there even two minutes before, as if she had made up her mind. Or perhaps she'd had it made up all along, and something he had said had only strengthened her resolve. She lifted the lid on the range and poked at the burning wood. The fire flared and died to hot coals again. She put in another stick of cottonwood and replaced the lid and stood there, as if warming herself.

"If I fight them, they'll know they've been fought," she said at last. "The Diemerts and Galts are fighters when they have to be."

It struck him how mannish her words sounded, though in truth he'd never heard a man say such things with such quiet resolve. There was no bravado about her, only utter determination. A man would boast and blow and try to do by bluff what he'd rather not do by action, but not this woman. She was scared to death, yet not so frightened that she could not act.

The cowboy had played her well, building on her fears until the last moment when he had threatened the children. It was a performance in a way—every bit as much a performance as the ones the traveling actors' troupes put on in Kansas City for the rich ladies and gentlemen. And it was a performance well done, built to the exactly appropriate and chilling climax.

The only thing the cowboy had not reckoned on was this woman.

Here she stood in the gloom of her 'dobe house, replaying that performance in her mind, and rather than terrifying her, it was infuriating her. Only cold anger and fierce determination would be left to harden her heart when she was finished.

Alvarez felt an urge to comfort her, to offer her solace, but of course that would be wrong. He had offered sound advice that she would not take, and now everything rested on her shoulders. Whatever happened to her, she would have it no other way than that she face it herself. Alone.

He admired her immensely.

"May I have some more coffee, please, Mrs. Diemert?" he asked after a time, mostly to break the self-imposed spell they each were falling under.

She jumped a little, as if startled, but her composure returned instantly.

"Of course."

He waited until she had poured the cup full and had sat down with him again.

"So you'll face them."

"I believe so."

"And the children?"

"They'll do what they have to do."

He tried to choose the next words carefully; they needed saying even though they would only deepen her anger and prevent the very thing they argued for.

"They will not be safe here, Cora. They're very small. We don't know yet what's happened to Joe."

She trembled a little in the darkness, but her voice displayed no emotion at all.

"The Lord will provide."

It was pointless. "I suppose so," he said.

Cora Diemert's steadfast resolve was nevertheless shaken when Joe and Billy Shingleton dragged themselves into the yard a few minutes before midnight that night. Shingleton's face was swollen so badly that one eye was shut entirely and the other not much more than a slit; Joe was so tired that no sooner had he stumbled into the house than he simply collapsed in front of the stove in a deep sleep. Cora had to help him to bed.

Shingleton sat at the table while Cora heated up some coffee, then he took the cup and left the house without a word to Alvarez; a few minutes later, Cora followed him outside.

Alvarez, guessing what it was they would be talking about, hobbled around the little house, delaying going outside. Better that she and Shingleton have a few minutes alone. He was too nervous to sleep anyway, as he always was when the certainty of violent action was upon him. Tonight, if he slept at all, it would be with one eye open.

Tonight, he had three enemies—a bad leg, Billy Shingleton, and a pack of land-hungry cowboys bent on destruction.

* * *

Cora carried a bucket of cold water from the tank beneath the windmill to the shed. Billy had stripped to the waist, and she set about ministering to his wounds by the light of a small lamp. She tore up a piece of rag and dipped it in the cold water and dabbed gently at the deep scrapes and bruises on his chest and shoulders and face. The abrasions would heal quickly, but the nose was badly broken; Billy had to breathe through his mouth because of the swelling and the clotted blood. She laid a piece of rag across the bridge of his nose. He didn't flinch, but he squinted the one open eye a little; amid the dull ache of his facial injuries, the nose was a sharp pain.

Still, she knew his deepest pain was the embarrassment.

He told her of the cowboys and how he'd lost the mule and the wagon, and she told him of the appearance of the foreman that day. Neither of them had to explain what all of it meant.

"Maybe I can ride in to Wagon Mound tomorrow," he said at last. "Or maybe you should. You and the girls can all ride that big horse, and Joe will have the other mule. Put the kids up in town and get some help. Or just take the kids and keep riding." He tried to smile.

She was silent for a long time. "You sound like the marshal," she said at last. "That would be his advice, too. I think we should give him his guns back."

Billy jerked as if he'd been shot. The wet bandage fell from his nose. "He's dangerous, Cora!"

"Not to me. Maybe to you, but not to me. He wanted to help me today when that cowhand came. He's a good man, Billy. I know it."

"He's the law!"

She wrung out another rag and laid it across a nasty welt on his shoulder. "And you aren't." The words dropped into the cool summer night air like stones into a still pool.

"Maybe you should ride in to Wagon Mound," he said again, halfheartedly.

"I'll not run."

"No, I reckon you won't, Cora. Too stubborn for your own good. Just don't forget your young 'uns."

She wiped cool water across his chest and felt him shiver, though she knew it wasn't from the cold. Her own hand began to tremble, and she had to fidget with her hair for a moment to bring herself under control.

"Are you afraid, Billy?"

He tried to grin without much success. "A little. For you, mostly. For me, some."

"Because of the marshal?"

"That. And the cowboys. More them than him. They'd just as soon have killed me and Joe out there. Might have, too, if it weren't that our coming back would give you a big scare. They're cowards, but that won't hold 'em forever."

"No. I know they'll be back."

"Then why don't you leave, Cora?" he asked. He gripped both her arms as he pleaded.

She tried to read his good eye in the half-light. Maybe it was only wishful thinking that saw the warm flash of love there.

Fear and love, existing side by side. The flash of recognition stunned her, for it was a similar combination of fear and love that had seemed to strangle her for almost as long as she could remember. Fear of leaving her beloved Missouri; fear of the wastes of the Indian Territory; fear of this half-desert plain; fear of the cowboys; and the love for her family that was really a fierce combination of pride and determination and sorrow. Perhaps fear and love equaled strength.

In this moment, crouching beside Billy Shingleton in the shed, she couldn't help but feel that this young man had joined her family in a way she couldn't begin to explain in words. And he felt it, too.

He took the wet rag off his nose again.

"Cora, I reckon you're right. You'd best give the marshal his weapons back. We brought back his big Smith and Wesson that Joe took."

"Why are you changing your mind?"

"Because we'll need all the gunhands we can get."

She played with her hair again, and her voice cracked when she spoke. "You're free to go to Wagon Mound . . . or wherever . . . before I give him his guns."

He grinned, and the crinkling of his face forced a thin trickling of blood from his nose.

"No," he said, "You'll need everyone, and I can handle a gun, too. Even with one eye. Those cowboys won't be playing games this time."

"But you could get away."

He shrugged. "What the hell. I got nowhere to go, anyway. It's either stay here or go back to Kansas with Tom Alvarez."

"But your brothers?"

"They won't be waitin'."

"You won't go back with the marshal."

"No, you're right. I won't. But I won't add murder of a federal officer and horse theft to my sins. Not now."

"You're a good man, Billy."

He reached out and took her hand. She stiffened. but didn't pull it away.

"Sometimes I'm all right, I reckon. But if them cowboys put me under, don't go looking for me to show up in heaven." Then, with the gentlest of tugs, he pulled her to him and kissed her once, tenderly.

It was already two in the morning; in just a few hours, day would be breaking.

Tom Alvarez was drinking the last of the coffee as she got ready for bed. He could see her form through the blanket she'd hung to drape off the beds from his view. She was slim and womanly, and not uncomely. In another time . . .

She pulled the drape aside once she was in her nightshirt and robe. The coal-oil light spilled across the room and onto Tom Alvarez. He didn't stir, and she guessed at once that he'd been watching her. The package wrapped in oilskin that she'd brought in from outside was still on the table where she'd left it, within his reach.

Cora brought the lamp with her to the table and unwrapped the package. The Smith and Wesson's nickel plating gleamed in the yellow light. She took the heavy, oddly balanced weapon in her hands and hefted it, her thumb across the hammer and her finger inside the trigger guard.

"There aren't any bullets in it. Not yet. But when the time comes, there will be," she said, laying the weapon carefully on the oilcloth.

His eyes met hers.

"Good night, marshal."

He nodded and rose and stumped outside. She could hear the sound of his crutch on the hard ground as he crossed the yard and headed for the shed he would share with Billy Shingleton for what was left of the night.

She went to her chair and laid the Bible in her lap and opened it to read the Psalms for a few minutes before she blew out the lamp.

CHAPTER 16

McALESTER was in a bad mood. They were as nervous as cats as he lined them up in the gray, predawn light, and that made him unhappy. After their attack on the man and the boy, they'd broken off their own roundup and come back to camp as they should, but some of them had spent the night drinking, and that made him furious. They'd taken on the stranger and the boy out on their pathetic little roundup purely for the hell of it, and now they were using the task before them as an excuse to get drunk. This thing that needed doing wasn't cause to celebrate, nor would it be any easier to accomplish if even one of the men wasn't fully capable of following orders.

He rode down the line, giving each man in his turn the once-over. Rawley seemed all right, though McAlester found the kid's enthusiasm more than a little troubling; killing was acceptable when it was necessary, but it shouldn't be enjoyable. The others were fidgety, but at least they were sober enough to keep their seats—all, that is, except for one kid who was new to the drives. McAlester ordered Swisher, the cook, to fill him up on the coffee that was left in the pot. Thick sludge, grown cold, might soak up enough cheap whiskey to keep him in the saddle farther than the edge of the camp.

"C'mon, boss!" Rawley called out loudly enough for all of them to hear. "We ain't goin' to get the drop on 'em if we ride in there in broad daylight. Let's go!"

McAlester formed a rebuke, but the words died before crossing his lips.

"Then lead on, Rawley," was all he said.

The kid waved his hat in the air like some smart-assed showman and spurred his horse into a canter, and the rest of the ragged line moved out after him.

McAlester brought up the rear himself, and after a while all he could see of the camp was the dim red glow of dying embers from the cooking fire and the dark form of the chuckwagon against the mottled graying in the east.

Clouds had moved in during the night, bringing with them a touch of coolness and dampness to the coming day, an oddity for this time of year. Still, this was the desert: the chances were that the brilliant late-summer sun would burn the moisture out of the sky, leaving only a high, thin scattering of clouds before noon.

Noon. McAlester strained his eyes to read the face of his pocket watch. Four-thirty. Not quite, but almost.

He hoped it would all be over by noon.

Damn, he thought to himself as he rode. And double damn. *Rawley's got the right attitude about this thing, after all, and I'm wrong.* The Millers and the Chisums and all their kind would surely agree with the kid on this one. Squatters are like mice in a flour bin. If you leave 'em alone, there'll be ten next year where there were two this year, but clean 'em out, and they stay cleaned out. Squatters got no right to the land—at least they got no right to go carving it up and fencing it in so a cowman can't run his herd. These people think they're cowmen, too, but they're just sod-busters at heart—two-bit cattle grazers who won't do anything more than bring bad bloodlines onto the range. And the real sod-busters will follow them, bringing their plows and draft horses and pigs and bobwire. Land this poor won't support sod-busters, but they'll ruin the range for everyone before they figure it out. They'll drive out the squatters who think they're "ranching," and they'll run the big operations out of business with their wire and law and courts and complaints.

No doubt about it. It all starts with these damn squatters.

So, first you warn them. Give them a chance to get off the

land to go somewhere more sensible for their kind. Then you scare hell out of them. And if that doesn't work . . .

He rode by the young kid, who had dismounted to urinate into a mesquite bush.

"Coffee runs right through you, don't it?" McAlester said as gruffly as he could.

"Yessir," the kid said without turning his head.

"Well, you best not wake up a sleepin' rattler, or we'll have to cut your pecker off to save your life!" McAlester laughed softly to himself. It was nerves, not coffee. Hell, he could stand to go himself. He turned half around in the saddle to check on the supplies he'd brought along.

Sixty feet of new hemp rope. Two big boxes of shells, both .44s and 30-06s—spares in case the boys used up what they carried on their own. Two gallon cans of kerosene.

Not much of a list, but it would do, as it had done before.

Billy Shingleton splashed at his face with the last of the cold water in the bucket she'd brought to tend to his bruises. His face still hurt, and the one eye was stuck shut. He worked at it with a sleeve to loosen the dried sleep that held the lids together. The nose felt some better, too, but he couldn't begin to breathe through it.

The sky was lightening, but it wasn't exactly daylight yet, not with the clouds. He pulled on his shirt and stuffed his revolver into his trousers before he ventured outside the shed. This morning, unlike most recent mornings, he surveyed the horizon all around the little homestead before he stepped away from the sheltering walls. For once, Tom Alvarez was not his chief concern.

He knew in his bones that this was the day—the morning—they would come. He'd been a bully long enough to know just how they thought.

For the first time since he could remember, the prospect of a fight sent a chill up his spine. He was afraid, but not just for himself. The odds were that several of them would die in this fight, Cora among them.

He wondered if what he felt for Cora was really love.

It was certainly different from the way he'd loved the silly young girls of home, those frilly things that teased and pouted in public and then were only too happy to lay with him in their daddies' haylofts. Those girls had been ladies-in-training, child-women who would do and dare anything so long as their parents and their high-tone gentlemen callers didn't find out. He'd been like a three-year-old colt with them, and of course that was all they'd wanted. In the moments when he'd allowed himself to imagine something like a normal life, free of his brothers and the gangs and the trouble, he'd sometimes thought of settling down with one of those young girls, but the thought always made him uncomfortable; surely in time they'd grow to be like their mothers, cold and shrill and overweight from too many children and too many dumplings and biscuits, too much gravy and buttermilk. He'd decided then to spread his seed, to enjoy the fillies, and not wait around for them to grow old and fat and bossy.

Cora Diemert was so different from any of them. From the very first, he had thought that she reminded him of his mother, but now he knew that it wasn't his mother at all that he saw in her. Rather, it was the strength and resolve he had always admired in strong men outside his family—traits he'd despaired of finding in women. Only a handful of people he had known in his life had had such strength, and she was the first woman. He was drawn to that strength as a needle is to a magnet. Even the animal lust had diminished in the face of this strength of character, or had been transformed into something deeper and more worthy of time and nurturing. He imagined himself with her, but only on her terms, at a time and place and in a way of her choosing. He cared for her, as a woman and as a friend.

Perhaps it *was* love.

And now she was in mortal danger. Now, he knew, there would be no time.

He scanned the eastern and southern approaches to the ranch with special care, but there was nothing to be seen.

A thin wisp of smoke rose from the chimney straight into the still air, and he could smell bacon and eggs frying. He went to the door but waited a moment before knocking. Tom Alvarez was already inside, and he was laughing.

The little girls had awakened as soon as Alvarez came in, and they'd stared so soberly at him, their faces perfect mirrors of their mother's, that the marshal had decided to perform for them. Joe just scowled from his bed with his legs dangling over the side as Alvarez's tricks set his sisters to giggling.

Taking his bandana, Alvarez had covered his hands and drawn the corners of the cloth up between two fingers, making what looked like a blue rabbit's head that he now had nibbling at the girls' fingers as they waited for their breakfast. They reached for the rabbit, but he kept it just beyond their grasp, and they laughed with delight at the game. Nettie, the little one, was especially entranced by the way the blue bandana rabbit darted in to touch her and then away when she reached for it. Alvarez refolded the handkerchief into a new toy, a mouse with a fat body and a long tail and two small ears where he'd tied a knot in the corner. By flipping it with his fingers, he could make the mouse jump up his forearm and away from Nettie. The girl laughed again.

Alvarez couldn't help thinking of his own childhood, that dimly remembered time when his own grandfather had played these same games—games he'd forgotten until now. God knows, he'd been too much like young Joe—too serious, too much in a hurry to grow up. But boys were like that, or at least they were when they had to be, and Joe Diemert had to be.

"You know how to shoot a gun, boy?" he asked without pausing in the game with the girls.

Lydia, perhaps sensing the importance of the question, grew serious suddenly, but Alvarez made the mouse jump, and Nettie squealed with glee.

"Yessir. Some," the boy said grudgingly.

"Shingleton teach you?"

Joe frowned and looked at his toes and didn't answer.

"Well, if he did, it's a good thing."

Cora rattled the cast iron skillet. "Men always think it's a good thing when boys learn how to shoot and kill."

"Comes in handy once in a while, that's all."

She scooped the eggs onto the platter that already held crisp curls of bacon, the last she had. "I suppose. Now you girls leave the marshal alone and set the table so's we can eat."

"Yes'm," Lydia said. She tugged at her little sister's sleeve, and Alvarez obligingly unwrapped the bandana and stuffed it back into his pocket.

He stood and leaned all his weight on the bad leg. There was a deep ache to it; without the splints and crutch he wouldn't be able to use it at all. Still, the sharp, overwhelming pain was past. Deep inside, the bone was knitting. He hobbled to the table and picked up his Smith and Wesson in its well-oiled holster. The weight and feel of it as he strapped it against his good thigh was a comfort, as if the power in the weapon counterbalanced the weakness and vulnerability in him now that he was a cripple. Even empty, the revolver was a good and trusted friend.

"You'll not wear that at table, Marshal," Cora said.

"No, ma'am. I plan to go outside for a while. You and the children . . . and Mr. Shingleton . . . go ahead without me. I'll just take a cup of coffee."

"But . . ."

He smiled broadly, the wide slit of his mouth under the hawk's-beak nose showing his good, strong teeth. "A man gets used to not eating, ma'am." What he wasn't going to tell her was that a hungry man had sharper senses, somehow: a hungry man was more efficient in a fight, saw more clearly, and was more able to concentrate on the thousand things that need concentration than a man made sluggish by a full belly. Before she could argue, he hobbled to the door and threw it open. Shingleton stood thirty feet away. He was watching the rim of hills and the cut near the mesa.

"Breakfast, Billy," Alvarez called out as he stumped out to stand next to the younger man.

Shingleton turned slowly. He twitched when he saw the gun at Alvarez's side, but he made no move to his own pistol.

"She's made a good breakfast for you, boy," Alvarez said quietly. "Only go easy so's you don't get drowsy later."

"I ain't hungry. You eat mine."

"No. I'll stand my turn watching."

"Why? So you can get the drop on me?"

Alvarez spat into the dust. "I figure we're in it together now. At least for a while. You could have got away, but you stayed. I'm stuck with a bum leg, and the woman ain't leaving. So go have some breakfast, dammit."

Billy looked at him in the gray predawn. He started to say something but stopped, and Alvarez hawked phlegm and spat again. Satisfied at last, Billy began to move toward the door. Alvarez's big hand swung up and caught him at the elbow.

The marshal's voice was low and urgent. "I need bullets for my piece, boy. You get 'em now, before you eat." Alvarez furrowed his brow; his deep-set eyes became invisible to Billy. He squeezed the elbow hard.

"Why the hell should I? I'm bossin' this thing, Marshal, not you." Shingleton jerked his arm free and turned his back on Alvarez, but the next words stopped him cold.

"You're going to need a steady hand with a gun before this day is over, never mind what's between you and me. You know that as well as I do, or you wouldn't have been standing here waiting for 'em to come. If somebody here's got to take dead aim on a man, let's have it be you and me, not that kid. If you let that boy go to man-shooting, you're killing him as sure as the cowboys will."

The hot blood of anger rose in Shingleton's face. He started to say something, but the words failed to come, and slowly the anger faded. The look left in its place said all that needed saying between them.

Alvarez was right.

Billy Shingleton wasn't bossing this thing. Not any longer.

"Now, give me a chamberload of bullets, Billy, and go eat your breakfast with Cora."

McAlester drew them up on the east side of the mesa. Even from here, a good eye could make out the thin streamer of smoke rising straight into the brightening sky. The Diemert ranch was less than a quarter mile away.

The boys saw it, too, and were quiet.

He wondered if any of them were praying. It seemed appropriate to say a prayer for strength and wisdom. For a few seconds, he tried to pray himself, but a man got out of the habit, and on reflection, maybe this wasn't a thing God could be called upon to help in, anyway.

"How do we go from here, boss?" Rawley asked quietly. The itch for action seemed to have left him now, though McAlester suspected that it was only temporary. Once he saw the quarry . . .

McAlester pointed to Rawley and the green young kid who had managed to stay in the saddle after all. "You two stay with me, here in the center. Two others ride north and climb to the top of this mesa. Position yourselves a couple hundred yards past the house. There's some gullies over there you can use for cover when we move in. The rest ride around west about a half mile. There are some low hills there." He pulled out his pocket watch. "I'll give everyone fifteen min-

THE INTRUDERS ■ 161

utes to get where they're going. Find what cover you can, and when you hear me start shooting, be ready. Pick your targets carefully, and don't waste ammunition. Use the long guns. Revolvers won't do nothing but make your ears ring. And I'm rationin' the ammunition. If you need bullets, send someone back to me for more. And for God's sake, keep low. That stranger you rousted with the boy yesterday is a hell of a shot."

"When do we charge the place?" the green kid asked.

"You'll know. I've got the fire here." He patted the kerosene cans. "Just stay as high in the hills or on the mesa as you can and still get a shot. I don't want anyone hurt by our own bullets. It's one thing to catch them in a cross-fire, but it's another to catch ourselves."

"That's it?" the kid asked. He was all business now. Too much, McAlester thought. Too serious to be sober. How the hell had the kid managed to sneak a bottle along?

"That's it. You've got fifteen minutes," he said.

He and Rawley waited as dawn came and the first red slice of the sun rose over the blue-gray plain far to the east. The air was warming quickly, as he had known it would; by the time the sun reached its zenith, it would be hot. McAlester checked the watch often—so often that he betrayed the nervousness creeping up his spine and making his heart beat hard enough to feel in his throat. He'd done this before, but somehow it had never been quite like this. Perhaps it was because he'd done it too often. Or because they were going against a woman. A woman with young children.

Nits. That's what Chisum had called them in the old days. Nits, pure and simple. Pests that had to be exterminated before they grew into adults and squatted on even more of the open plains.

Still . . .

He remembered the first time they'd driven out a bunch of nesters. He was still working for Chisum then, before

Rudy Miller had taken him on. Two Scotsmen it was then, a pair of crazy bastards who'd taken over a Chisum line shack on the range south of the ranch, along the bend in the Pecos where it swung east toward Texas. That had been a long time ago, back in '76 or '77, even before the Lincoln County troubles. Old Man John Chisum had ridden with them himself to take care of the Scotsmen, and they'd done it without too much trouble. They'd set fire to the shack, and when the two men had finally come out gagging and choking from the smoke with their hair singed off and their hands held high, they'd tied them up and thrown them over pack saddles like so many sacks of flour.

They'd found the tree they wanted about a mile away. The men were already half beaten to death from bouncing against the rough saddles, but they'd found breath enough to plead for their lives. McAlester and the others had laughed at them and mocked their brogue, and they'd strung them up without so much as a fare-thee-well. Only after they were dead, when their faces had gone black and their swollen tongues had come popping out of their open mouths, had the awfulness of the deed struck him and all of them who had been a part of it; it was a long time before they could ride that stretch of the Pecos without thinking about those two Scotsmen.

But John Chisum had paid each man ten dollars extra and a bottle of whiskey that month just so they'd remember who was in charge.

In spite of the whiskey and money, it hadn't gotten any easier in the intervening years. Nor, luckily, had it gotten to be very frequent. It hadn't taken too many lynchings in the Pecos country for the squatters to get the idea and clear out on their own.

Things didn't seem to be working that smoothly up here along the Canadian. Rudy Miller still found it easy enough to suggest the old solutions, but it was tougher now to discourage the nesters.

Maybe it was because Miller cattle were new to these northern grasslands, almost as new as some of the squatters. Maybe it was because there were so many of them now, come for the staying, for taking up the land. From his vantage point on this mesa, the country looked empty except for the Diemert place in the little hollow down below, but in reality the intruders were everywhere. The Pecos squatters had been cowboys mostly, men looking for a quick stake in the cattle business, usually by rustling heifers and unbranded calves from the bigger outfits. These were families moving in now, bringing their own herds with them, content to set up their homesteads as they fenced off a section and brought it to the plow. And fifteen years before, when the ranchers were just getting started to the south, these northern grasslands had still fed a large part of a great buffalo herd; McAlester knew deep in his soul that if this soil would grow something finer than bunch grass and prickly pear, then no power on earth would keep out the sod-busters for long.

The Diemerts might scare, but families brought other families, and no handful of cowhands could clean them all out. Before long, there'd be little ranches springing up on every arroyo, with kids and cows and chickens, just like the place they'd come to destroy this fine morning.

Before long . . .

"Ain't that fifteen minutes up yet, boss?" Rawley asked.

McAlester snapped open the tarnished silver case of the pocket watch once more.

It was time.

CHAPTER 17

ALVAREZ felt them coming even before the first shot spurted up sand at his feet. The hackles on the back of his neck had been crawling, and he'd strained his eyes scanning the mesas and the hills. Once he thought he saw movement, but the light was still too dim to be certain. Every part of his body throbbed with tension and anticipation.

So the spurt of sand, followed an instant later by the sharp report of the rifle, triggered him as a match did gunpowder. He drew his Smith and Wesson and limped backward, struggling to keep his feet as he made as big a stride as possible with the crutch.

He could lose no time: a second shot would be closer to the mark.

It came, with enough range to have struck him dead if it hadn't been wide; the slug thudded into the 'dobe wall of the little house.

"Look to your weapons!" Alvarez shouted to those behind him as he backed through the door. Instinctively, he began preparing their line of defense. "Shingleton, you run for the chicken coop so we can keep their aim split on two locations. It'll give you a better view." Other bullets, coming in rapid succession, smacked into the house, one splintering a chunk out of the door just as Alvarez pushed it shut.

He was suddenly aware that his heart was pounding in his throat and his leg hurt like sin.

"I can see 'em from here!" Shingleton said. He was already working at peeling back a corner of the greased paper.

"Not well enough," Alvarez said. "We're blind to the east and west both." His mind raced as he tried to think through all the hidden dangers so he could anticipate their attack. He was angry with himself for not working all this out sooner. Damn, but they *were* practically blind! And his leg hurt badly; the pain nagged at him, sapping his strength, making it so much harder to concentrate on the matters at hand. He pulled a chair over beside the door so he could sit down. "Cora, you and the children keep down as low as you can. Under the table, maybe."

"I see 'em!" Shingleton said, and he stuck his rifle through the window and squeezed off a shot.

"They'll come at us from the sides," Alvarez said. "You make a run for the chicken coop and I'll cover you."

"The hell with you, Alvarez. You can't give me orders." He stuck the gun barrel out the window and fired again.

"Quit wasting powder!" Alvarez snapped.

"I can shoot," Joe said, a little too loudly.

A new volley of shots thudded into the house, and one tore through the window six inches from Shingleton's head.

He squeezed off another aimless shot.

"It'll be like shooting fish in a barrel unless we get a set of eyes outside!" Alvarez said. "You have to go, Billy."

Shingleton shot him a scowl. "I ain't leaving Cora defenseless. You can't even move!"

"Oh, stop it, you two!" Cora said. She was herding both girls toward their beds. Wide-eyed terror filled their faces. She sat them on the floor and upended her small reading table to shield them. Like fawns retreating to the sheltering side of their mother, they did as she bid them.

"I can shoot," Joe said again, screaming to be heard over the whine and rattle of the steady firing peppering the house. Another bullet tore through the door: too spent to hurt anyone, it clattered against the stove.

Alvarez shifted his weight in the chair and eased the door open a crack. He could sight over the hinges, but his field of view was only a few degrees wide. He looked quickly at

Shingleton's position to judge how well he could see. The torn corner of the window wouldn't be much better.

"Billy, one of use has to go out there, and I can't make it with his leg."

"I'm staying. Cora needs protection." He stood up tall, placing his body directly between Cora and Alvarez as if to prove his point.

"I'm not your enemy, boy," Alvarez said, the fatigue suddenly showing in his voice. "The best thing you can do is give us a pair of eyes to see what they're doing!"

Shingleton scowled at him, but slowly his face twisted with the realization that Alvarez was right. On both counts. One of them had to get outside, at least to the shed, for a better vantage point. The attackers would be spread out over a broad front, and there was nothing to keep them from sneaking up from the rear. And Billy himself was the only one who had any chance to get to other cover without being cut down.

He spat on the floor. Alvarez watched him make up his mind.

Shingleton stepped across the room to the door and turned and slid the rifle to Cora. "I've got his rifle outside with my truck," he said. Then he faced the door and sucked in a deep breath, steeling himself for the long run.

"Keep low and keep moving," Alvarez said.

"To hell with you, Marshal," Shingleton said between his teeth as he flung the door wide open and ran out into the red glow of early morning.

Alvarez fired now for the first time, three shots in quick succession followed by three more, emptying his gun in the direction of the unseen enemy. Cora, seeing now what had to be done, scooped up the rifle and rammed the muzzle through the opening in the window and aimed high, toward the mesa, and fired until the carbine was empty.

"I'm reloaded," Alvarez said through the choking blue

gunsmoke that filled the little house. He shouted at the top of his lungs: "Billy! You make it?"

For a long moment there was no answer. Inside, no one breathed, and the sudden silence was awful. And then they heard Billy whoop, followed by the crack of his revolver.

"Damn! We need another long gun!" Alvarez said more to himself than anyone else.

"I can shoot," Joe repeated plaintively from his place beside the stove.

McAlester cuffed the young cowboy on the back of the head, sending the kid sprawling. The first two shots, utterly wasted, had only warned the squatters that the battle was at hand. He'd told the kid to take aim for the big man on the crutch, who should have been easy pickings; but buck fever had taken hold and now it was too late to cut the opposition in half with one quick shot. McAlester cursed himself for not shooting the man himself, but he cuffed the kid again just to make sure he got his point across.

Rawley had gotten his windage quickly, and he was peppering the adobe house and making his shots count as well as he could at the distance. When he stopped to reload, McAlester heard the first fire coming from the other boys, now well into position on either side of the place.

But the adobe would hold for as long as they wanted to pour lead into it. The people might weaken, frighten, and give up. But the adobe would hold against gunfire. Their best chance was to get close, to use the fire that could drive the squatters into the open where his boys could pick them off leisurely.

God, he'd hoped it wouldn't come to that. If the kid had made that first shot work, it wouldn't have, either. McAlester had seen enough gunfights to know that a quick killing shot that crippled the opponent's ability ot fight always brought victory, and often an easy one. But momentum was everything; now, neither side had any, and it might be a long day of shooting, the squatters and his boys plinking at each other. The cowboys were in good formation, with three separate positions bearing down on the little house, but the adobe was thick. And perhaps more importantly, the woman had already proven her nerve.

He looked at the kerosene cans.

Maybe Mrs. Diemert and the two men with her didn't have much ammunition. If he could get them to waste as much as possible of whatever they had, then he still might be able to end it without risking the boys who would have to Indian-crawl up to the place to pour the kerosene.

To get them to waste ammunition meant wasting his own. Pepper the soddy to make them nervous enough to shoot at dust and tumbleweeds and anything that moved. His own nerves were already frayed.

"Damn!" Rawley shouted through the thin haze of gun-smoke and the ringing of gunfire in their ears. "Get him. Get him! Damn, don't miss him!"

McAlester peered in the direction that Rawley was pointing and saw Shingleton dash for the shed behind the main house. Bullets whizzed and spurted dust at the man's feet, but somehow he reached his goal, apparently unhurt. And then suddenly dust and sand flew into their own faces and behind them a horse whinnied crazily.

Jesus!

McAlester whirled, half-expecting to find the Diemert woman and some ally who had crept up behind them.

A horse had taken a bullet in the ribs. It was a spent bullet—had to be, because the horse was standing a little below them—but it had brought a trickle of blood and frightened the horse so badly that it reeled and jerked against the picket stake.

Blind rage seized McAlester. He whipped out his revolver and shot the horse once in the neck. It plunged, broke the short rope, stumbled, and fell. He cursed the horse and shot it again and then a third time. It twitched just once before it died.

"Jesus, Mac!" It was Rawley, gripping his arm, trying to pry the revolver out of his hand. "Jesus, Mac, that's your horse!"

McAlester spun and he raised his gun above his head, ready to strike at whatever got in his way. But the fury passed as quickly as it had come. His scattered thoughts refocused in an instant.

Panic. Rage and panic.

"How the hell did that cowboy get away from us?" was all he could say.

"I ain't sure, but I think we winged him. I got off a good shot."

"He looked all right to me."

"I ain't sure."

"Why the hell can't we hit 'em?" McAlester asked again. He felt the panic rising in his throat once more, but it shamed him and he fought it down.

"I don't know, boss. But keep your head down. They're shootin' back."

A thin, humorless smile came to McAlester's face. "That's damned obvious, boy, unless we're shooting backwards!" He jerked a thumb over his shoulder at the dead horse. "Go get the mounts down lower where some damn stray bullet can't get to 'em . . . or where I can't get to 'em if something sets me off again."

The blue haze and the smell of burnt gunpowder on the overheated air inside the little adobe house was suffocating. In the moments of pause, Cora fought off an urge to gag. She longed to throw the door open for a cooling breeze or just fresh air. Then she'd hear the splat of a bullet as it splintered the heavy wood of her door, and a split second later there would be the report, the sharp crack that the bullet itself had outrun. Her heart pounded at the murderous sounds, and every muscle in her body ached for flight. Yet she stood beside Tom Alvarez.

Stood her ground. Yelled at her children to keep low. Pleaded with Joe to watch out for the girls.

Reloaded. Fired.

Stood her ground.

Alvarez laid out the ammunition on the floor and divided it into two piles, a small one and a large one.

"We use up the bigger stack now. Shoot only when there's a target, but shoot if you have to," he said as he reloaded the Smith and Wesson. The chamber and barrel were so hot he could hardly touch them.

"What about the other?"

"We save it."

"What for?"

He snapped the cylinder into place and then looked at her, the cold steel blue of his eyes boring into her.

"For the last," he said.

And she understood.

Shingleton propped himself up at the very back of the shed, in the deep shadows where he could look out into the yard without being seen. From there, he could see both the rise where the main force of the attackers was hidden and the higher point on the mesa where the first shots had come from. There were others, off to his right, but he would have to give up on being able to keep his eyes on them. He'd have to trust his instincts. For now.

His thigh pained him. God, he wished suddenly for a drink of good Kentucky whiskey.

The bullet had torn into his leg when he was just two strides short of the safety of the shadows. It had felt like a deep, probing hornet's sting at first; only when he'd sat down, only when the burning had welled up throughout his body, making his stomach turn, had it dawned on him fully that he'd been shot.

He tried to inspect the wound by pulling the blood-soaked cloth away from the hole.

The bullet was lodged in the big muscle of the back of his leg, just a few inches below the buttocks. He couldn't see it very well no matter how he twisted his body. The bleeding was steady, but he could see no spurting of bright blood, either, so some of his old luck had held: no artery was severed.

He tore off his bandana and jammed it against the wound and sat down so all his weight was on it. The leg was stiffening already.

God, but he hoped that would work. If it didn't, he'd have to use whatever rope he could find to rig a tourniquet between his groin and hip. The thought crossed his mind that he could lose the leg.

But then he laughed and gave another piercing yell like the old Reb boys did on the Fourth of July back home.

He dug around in his gear until he found Alvarez's long gun and what ammunition he had. He loaded quickly and laid the rifle across his lap.

"Come on, you bastards!" he said aloud. "Come on and let's all go to hell together!"

"We got to rush 'em soon, boss, or we got a Mexican standoff. We can shoot that house up till doomsday and not hurt 'em."

McAlester considered Rawley's advice silently, with only a slight frown. *Of course,* he thought. *Any damn fool can tell that. Isn't that what I've been thinking myself for the last half hour?*

"The boys on the west flank are letting us down," was all he chose to say after a time. "They've got a clear shot at getting in closer, what with those folks being blind from that side."

"Then let's send the kid over there an' get 'em movin'!" Rawley shouted.

McAlester eyed him coldly.

"You go, Rawley."

The younger man's face darkened with blood.

"I mean it. You go. I'm putting you in charge of that flank. Push in on 'em hard as you can. You ought to be able to get right up to the house. We'll open up a fusillade and you can move in at will." The cold grin came to his mouth again, but not his eyes. It promised anger and a threat of violence.

Rawley hawked phlegm and spit it into the dust at his feet. He started to say something, then decided against it. Spinning on one heel, he loped off to the west, to take up his new command.

McAlester called to him to stop.

"Take these!" he shouted, and he held two gallon cans of kerosene aloft. Rawley grinned and came back for them and was gone.

McAlester was sorry that he couldn't buy more time.

But why did he want more time? End it. Now. That's what he should be doing. The kerosene was the answer. But he wanted to wait. Maybe something in him wanted to be away from Rawley, too. Rawley. So much like McAlester himself **had** been once.

"You be ready to fire to cover him," he said to the kid. "And this time, don't screw it up!"

Tom Alvarez mopped the sweat out of his eyes.

There wasn't much time, and he knew it. He was still worried about the blind side. From what he could see from the house and what Shingleton ought to be able to see from the shed, the eastern and southern approaches to the Diemert place were covered. The west was blind, and some of the attackers were well to their west. Somehow, they had to get protection from that side as well.

"Can we chop a hole in the wall?" His voice was husky from thirst and the acrid air.

"It's a foot thick," Cora said.

"We've got to do something."

Joe stepped up between them. "I can shinny up through the chimney hole and keep watch from the roof."

"No, I told you," his mother said. "Now hush and keep still."

Alvarez looked at them both.

"It would help."

"I won't expose him to the danger!"

"I'll keep low, Ma."

"No!" But of course it was the only way.

Alvarez hobbled across the room and pulled the tin chimney away from the hole in the ceiling. She didn't try to stop him. A thin rain of soot and crumbled adobe sifted down into the smoky room. He and Joe pushed the table over to where the boy could crawl up the chimney. It sagged under his weight and threatened to buckle and Alvarez reached up to give him a boost. The boy squirmed up and poked his head out the small opening.

"They're on the west side near the tree," the boy said breathlessly as he dropped back onto the table.

The soft thump of bullets hitting the adobe behind the girls' beds confirmed it: the attackers were coming from the blind side. Since they'd been discovered, they had no reason to hide themselves now.

"Damn it!" Tom Alvarez said softly.

Cora Diemert stood beside him. Her fists were clenched so that the knuckles were white and tears stained her grimy cheeks, but she said nothing to castigate him for this new transgression.

Shingleton heard the firing begin. It was closer and on his right; he dragged himself to where he could see out between the slats in the side wall of the shed. The exertion brought fresh blood to the wound in his thigh, but it couldn't be helped.

There they were. His head throbbed from the beating of the day before and his eyes were still swollen, but he could see plenty well enough in spite of the swelling to take in the whole scene in a second.

Three cowboys, hunched over to keep low, coming toward the house. The nearest wasn't thirty yards away.

He aimed Alvarez's rifle carefully. A close target made it easy: the slug would drop little over that distance.

His target paused for an instant, and in that heartbeat, Billy squeezed off a shot.

The sound of the report reverberated in the shed, and the blue pungent smoke filled his eyes and nose, but he knew that he'd struck his mark. The high, thin yelp of pain was enough. He wiped his eyes with the back of his hand and took aim on a second cowboy who had stopped to lean over his friend.

Somehow, the next shot missed, and so did a third, but they sent the two cowboys sprawling for cover, leaving their downed friend where he had fallen.

Billy looked closely to see if the man moved. He didn't, and a fourth shot within a foot of the body brought no reaction. The first shot had done its work.

Now there was return fire. The two men still left sent several shots in his direction from their hiding places. One bullet splintered a slat inches from Billy's head. He fired once more to keep them down.

That was when he heard the fusillade from the far ridge to the south. Suddenly there were other rebel yells, more shots from the ridge, and a burst of gunfire from the house.

One of the two men to the west stood up, braving Shingleton's fire, and the other opened up on the shed, shattering more of the slats and sending lead and chunks of wood flying through the chicken roosts and the spot where Billy knelt. He tried to get a bead on the first man, but a bullet struck so near him that it drove slivers stinging into his face and drawing blood; for a second he thought he'd been hit by the bullet itself. He spun away, but not before he saw them, all of them, coming over the rise. On foot, zigzagging to keep away from Alvarez's bullets.

A few of them were carrying something. Awkwardly. Something that bumped into their legs as they ran.

"God!" he said as he wiped tears and blood off his cheek.

"Fire! Alvarez, they're gonna burn you out!" he shouted at the top of his lungs. There was other shooting at the house, and the big boom of a shotgun, but in spite of the din, he had to make them understand. "Fire! Watch out!" He dragged himself back to his hiding place in the shadows and reloaded. So they would come at them with coal oil, then be ready to cut them down in a cross-fire as soon as they were smoked out. "Fire, Cora!" he shouted again.

He watched the cowboys coming on, the ones with the heavy cans running abreast of the others.

He took up his rifle again and waited for them to get within range.

CHAPTER 18

CORA Diemert saw the cowboy the same instant that she heard Billy's shouted warning about the fire. She caught him in the sights of the shotgun as he was coming around the house, angling in for the door that stood partway open.

Without thinking, without considering what it meant, she pulled the triggers on both barrels.

The concussion knocked her backward, and the horrible ringing in her head matched the booming crash of the twelve-gauge.

Alvarez looked at her and said nothing. His face was smeared black with burnt powder, his eyes rimmed red with fire and pain. He allowed himself only a glance to decide that she was all right; other business needed seeing to now that the real assault had begun.

The other cowboys were still beyond effective range and might stay that way for a few minutes: they had seen what the shotgun blast had done to their friend and for now they had slowed down a little. He took a shot just to remind them of the danger, but he didn't waste another. At this distance, he could pepper them, make them a little more skittish, but a killing shot would be more luck than skill. And the ammunition was running low. He scooped up a handful of bullets so he'd be ready to reload in a hurry. There weren't three dozen rounds left between them, not counting whatever she had for the shotgun.

Alvarez stole a glance at the cowboy beyond the front door. His shirt was black with blood, and the dark stain was spreading around him in the sand.

"Why don't they stop? Why, Ma?" Joe cried from the

middle of the room where he stood, his head blackened from the chimney hole.

His mother said nothing.

"Why don't they stop, Ma?" This time, it was almost a whimper.

In the relatively quiet seconds between gunshots, Alvarez could hear the girls softly sobbing from their hiding places on the floor near the beds. He wished he could spare them, spirit them away from this awful place.

He shook his head to clear away the fatigue and focused his attention once again on the attackers.

A wiry young cowboy leading the assault had split off a couple of the others and sent them scurrying along the base of the rise toward the west. To take up where the dead cowboy had left off.

Alvarez tried a careful shot, but it only sprayed sand a few feet behind the runners. His guns were too hot and his hands no longer steady enough.

God, if he could only wing one or two more of them, maybe they'd give it up for a bad try. Too much to hope, maybe, but he'd hope nonetheless. Or if they got close enough, he could blast them with the shotgun, as she had. And why hadn't they been smart enough to come at night? Hell, they could have ridden right into the yard and burned them out with no one the wiser.

Oh, Lord, he was so tired, and his leg hurt.

The cowboys bunched together as if they were unsure of themselves or their leadership.

Maybe they're looking at that black stain spreading across the yard, he thought.

No. They were coming on. More from the east this time, but those other two were still working their way west, too.

He emptied his gun at them.

"You be ready with the shotgun, Cora. If they get close enough, send 'em straight to hell with it."

Rapid firing came from behind them. Shingleton was

firing; a cowboy dropped, hit. Not fatal, probably, but a good leg shot. The others hunkered down again, but they didn't have much cover now. They sent a volley of their own toward the chicken house.

Alvarez looked at Cora. She was pale as death. He stumped toward her, leaving the door open. Maybe he could comfort her somehow. She leaned heavily onto him, and he could tell from her breathing that she was crying. It was the heaving, strangled crying of uncontrollable rage, not fear.

"Save the buckshot, Cora," he said gently. "For the final assault. It'll do a powerful lot of good for us then."

More firing from Shingleton's direction, and from the attackers'.

"We're sure wasting . . ."

The boom of an ancient revolver interrupted him. For a split second he had no idea where the sound had come from, and then he knew. Alvarez whirled and saw Joe with the old gun held out in both hands at arms' length. Alvarez opened his mouth to shout, but before any sound would come, Joe cocked the big hammer again and pulled the trigger.

His target, gut-shot, stumbled through the door and fell, dropping a burning rag torch as he came. The flames licked at the doorpost.

Joe aimed lower and cocked the hammer again.

"No, son!" Cora screamed and tore away from Alvarez. The gun fell from the boy's hands and went off, the unaimed bullet slamming into the adobe a few inches from Alvarez's good leg.

The cowboy rolled over and tried to speak. Bright blood frothed out of his mouth. He looked incredibly young, surely no more than sixteen. He caught his breath once, but then no more; the youthfulness stayed on his face even after the color of life had begun to ebb away.

Alvarez shook himself out of his stupor. How could he have left the doorway when they were so close! He sucked in as much air as his lungs would hold and stepped over the body, positioning himself once more at the door, ready to do battle.

Cora grabbed Joe and dragged him to the window, his face buried in her skirt so he might not see the foulness of the death he had wrought.

"Stop it, damn you all!" she screamed at all of them. And then screamed it again. "For the love of God, stop!"

But even as she screamed, even as Joe held tight to her, she broke open the shotgun and pulled out the spent cartridges and loaded the two chambers again.

McAlester lay hugging the earth. He couldn't take his eyes off the bloodied corpse in front of the house, could neither bring himself to go on, nor to stop this thing. For a few moments, seconds really, they had had momentum on their side. And then carelessness—recklessness—had ended it. To see one of his hand-picked men, cut in half . . .

When the boys from the western flank had swung around the front of the house, McAlester could only close his eyes and wait for the inevitable. He heard the gunshots, first the blast of the shotgun and later the two separate revolver shots. And now two fine cowhands were surely dead.

Damn them, but why couldn't they wait? Splash the house with the kerosene, and *then* light the torches.

But they were all in a hurry.

He heard Rawley shouting orders, organizing another charge, sending one bunch in a sweep straight north so they could get around east of the house, out of range of the guns in the doorway. McAlester heard it, but did nothing to help his men or stop them.

Rawley was going now, he and the young kid who had ruined it all by firing too soon. Running crazily for the ranch. Shooting at everything. Wild Indians. Damned wild Indians.

You go. Get right up to the house. You can move in at will.

That's what he'd told Rawley. McAlester knew he was derelict for sending them off on this assault without better guidance than that. He should have led them himself. But he could not. He had no stomach for this business any longer.

Still, he forced himself to watch.

Momentum again. Maybe they had it. God, they were getting close.

Then firing again from that damned shed. Them returning fire, breaking stride, looking for nonexistent cover. Crazy fight. Rawley running again, this time for the shed, not the house.

Sure. Get behind them. One gun there, still two or three in the house. Sure. Take the one.

Shingleton watched them come on. Blood trickled into the corner of his mouth from the splinter cuts on his cheek. His trouser leg was wet to the ankle. He crawled to another spot where he could get better cover and still see them through the slats. Shivers took hold of him in spite of the heat of the day. He was awfully cold. Cold, but clearheaded enough to be ready for what was coming.

And that was the one they called Rawley, the big-mouth.

Shingleton needed a smoke. He forced himself to concentrate on other things. Reload Tom Alvarez's rifle. Keep his head down. His cartridges were almost gone. One or two more salvos, and he'd be firing dry.

Then he could have his smoke.

Billy Shingleton laughed out loud. He thought about the gold, buried out there where only he and Joe knew to find it. Funny how he didn't even want the money now. Just wanted to get out of this scrape, strike a deal with Alvarez, and get to Colorado. To live.

Just live.

Rawley zigzagged his way into the yard. Shingleton tried to get a good bead on him, but when he pulled the trigger, nothing happened.

Damn! Damn the gun for jamming!

Then Rawley was upon him, almost stumbling over him as he rushed into the darkness of the shed. He spun around, trying to see, but he couldn't make Billy out in the shadows.

Shingleton tried to fire again, and the click gave him away.

Rawley fell against the back wall and turned to face the deep shadows beyond the doorway, his short-barreled rifle aimed in Shingleton's direction. He fired once and levered another shell into the chamber.

"Why don't you kill me?" Rawley gasped as he squinted into the shadows. His chest heaved from the run.

And from the fear. Billy could smell it on him. Shingleton patted his revolver still snug in his waistband. This was close-in work, so to hell with the long gun. He threw the rifle away and Rawley's eyes followed the noise: he fired and cocked almost in one motion.

"Whyn't you kill me?" Rawley demanded again. He gritted his teeth and swung the rifle in a slow arc as he squeezed the trigger until the hot flash of the muzzle lit the shadows for a hundredth of a second, just long enough to show him where Shingleton lay. "Well now, you bastard, I'm goin' to kill you!" Rawley exulted and he started to cock the rifle again.

The report of Shingleton's short gun filled the tiny space between them. Rawley jerked the rifle upward, sending a shot up through the roof, and slumped over sideways, the front of his shirt suddenly soaked with fresh blood.

Shingleton laid the revolver in his lap and dug in his shirt pocket for his tobacco. The hot pain of the new wound spread through the left side of his body. His shoulder was smashed for sure. Maybe it was worse than that.

The tobacco was already sticky from his blood.

He laid a cigaret paper in his lap, poured some of the tobacco, picked out the wet lumps with his fingers, and did his best to roll a smoke one-handed. It was a pathetic little cigaret when he was done, more paper than tobacco and all bent to hell, but it would have to do. He fumbled in his pocket for a match and found one.

Funny, he thought as he struck the match against his trousers. How quiet it had gotten after all the shooting. Maybe it was over. Maybe he would get to Colorado after all. There was still that bastard Alvarez to get around, but maybe they could work something out. Just a couple of days to rest, and then he'd be good as new. Maybe he'd even ride out alongside Alvarez, both of them with bum legs.

He tried to laugh, but a sudden weakness made the world swim around him. His breathing was coming hard. Too hard. He didn't notice when the smoldering butt of the cigaret fell into the straw beside him. All he saw was dancing lights.

"Ma," he said softly. *"Cora."*

His ears rang. And then nothing.

Alvarez's head throbbed in the silence. The only sounds were the muffled sobs of the girls, who were still huddled near their beds, and the pop and rustle of the dying fire that he reckoned had consumed the shed. They must have gotten to Shingleton with the fire. The smoke drifted lazily across the yard in the afternoon sun, but the orange glow of the flames was gone, burnt out.

His lips were caked and cracked and his tongue felt as thick as a boot heel, but he wouldn't ask the woman for water. Not now. She'd done so well until her boy had done the killing; now she was slumped in her rocker, the shotgun cradled in her lap, her head down and her eyes closed. Even though he was certain she wasn't asleep, he would not disturb her. Besides, he had to keep watch, keep his eyes glued to the swale where last they'd seen the attackers. For a time he'd worried about the one who had gotten behind them, but no longer. The shots and the fire and then the silence told him enough about that.

He was bone weary, and the leg ached from hip to ankle.

But out there, the cowboys were tired and hurt, too. And scared. They'd left men—three, maybe, if Shingleton's shots had counted—dead as all hell, which would give them plenty to think about.

Alvarez rubbed the back of his hand across his dry and burning eyes and waited.

The afternoon slowly faded to gold and red, and finally to the deep violet of a late-summer evening. The first stars came out in the east, blue-white and shimmering in the lingering heat of the day.

Cora Diemert finally stirred herself to fetch a little food for her children, dry corn bread mostly, and a cup of water from the dipper. She was in shock, her movements heavy and mechanical. Alvarez refused the food she offered, but he gulped two dippersful of the brackish water. Still, he did not move from the doorway.

Outside, the whippoorwills awoke, and an early bat fluttered crazily across the yard.

The cowboys regrouped at the place where they had split up, not so much because they had planned to as because they didn't know what else to do. They drank from their canteens and rested a little. Three down for sure, and Rawley missing. Probably dead in the fire. And several others nursing lesser wounds.

They looked to McAlester, but their eyes fell away from him out of embarrassment for him and for themselves. One of them started to say something, but the sound of a human voice was so out of place, so strange, that he fell silent without finishing the sentence. Each of them wondered what to do next, and all of them feared the answer.

After full dark had fallen, McAlester broke a bottle out of his saddlebags and passed it around. There would be just a swallow or two for each of them, but it would have to do. For comfort and cheer and courage. There wasn't enough for forgetting.

"We goin' to starve them out, or what?" someone asked at

last, and all of them squatted quietly on their haunches, waiting for an answer.

McAlester lit a cigaret before he spoke.

"No," he said at last. "It's over." Then he grabbed a horse and swung up into the saddle and nudged the animal over the ridge toward the little house, leaving them all behind.

CHAPTER 19

McALESTER stopped the horse twenty yards from the door. No light spilled out of the little house into the yard to give away the positions of the people inside; even so he could feel their eyes boring into him. He knew just where the hawk-nosed man was standing, watching. There was no moon yet, and neither man had anything other than starlight to see by: McAlester, black on a tall black horse in a black yard—the other, even darker in the total shadow of the adobe.

How much lead and hatred we poured at each other today, and now it comes to this, McAlester thought.

His horse whinnied, and he heard the metallic click of a gun cocking.

He took a deep breath and drummed up the courage to speak, all the while expecting to see the muzzle flash and feel the stabbing pain of a bullet.

"I come for my boys. Then we're leaving."

Nothing happened. No bright flash, no explosion, no searing pain. Nothing.

"I've got dead here," he said softly, "and maybe wounded. Just let me take my boys, and we'll go."

There was no answer, but he could hear movement inside the house. The door hinges creaked a little, and at last the woman spoke. "Why should I believe you?"

"Because you won."

"You've got two men right there in front of you. They're dead."

"I know that. There's another around back. My boys had to leave him."

The door slammed and he waited for their decision. The

185

horse whinnied again, probably from the nearness of death. He stroked its neck. .

After a few minutes, he heard the door open again; even though he saw nothing, he knew the double barrels of her shotgun were pointed straight at him.

This time the hawk-nosed man spoke. "You get your man, mister. And I'll be right behind you."

McAlester circled carefully around the house. He could smell the blood of the two dead men in the front yard. The horse was balky, but he managed to hold it in check, to keep it moving slowly. Once around back, he stopped to get his bearings. He could make out the shape of the tree and the water tank against the star-filled western sky. The stark outlines of the livestock pens and the rubble of the burned-out shed were barely visible on his right. The shed, the last place he had seen Rawley.

He found the third boy. He dismounted and rolled the body over. By some miracle, it was still warm. The boy stirred a little, as if from sleep, and tried to say something.

"Shhh," McAlester whispered. He struggled to lift him, but there was no way he could get the wounded boy onto the horse. He shifted the dead weight so he could carry the boy in his arms.

From the deep shadows beside the house, he heard the man clear his throat.

"You get your man out of here," Alvarez said.

"He's alive," McAlester said. "At least I think so."

"Fine. Get him out of here."

McAlester stood in the yard, considering. Then he adjusted the weight and turned and began walking back toward the ridge, letting his horse follow at will.

The woman called after him when he was well past the house.

"I'm not leaving here, mister! You can come again and again, but I'm not leaving! Never!" Her voice cracked, and he heard the shotgun clatter onto the hard dirt just outside the door.

McAlester walked a few steps more and stumbled in the sand and stopped to catch his breath.

"Just keep walking," Alvarez said from a few yards behind him. "Then come back for the others. Alone."

"That might take all night."

"If it takes all night, it takes all night."

The first sliver of moon crept up over the eastern horizon; soon enough, the people in the house would be able to pick their targets almost as well as in daylight.

McAlester turned around to face the house, the boy cradled in his arms. "All right," he said. "I'll come back for the others. Then we'll leave. You have my word, for what it's worth to you."

"I also want your weapons. I'm United States Marshal Thomas Alvarez from Kansas, and I want your weapons."

McAlester couldn't help a dry laugh. "Hell, Marshal, this is pretty rough country. We'll need our guns."

"Then leave the rifles. You can keep the revolvers."

"No."

"Then I guess we'll keep your friends."

"I can't go rounding up my boss's cattle without rifles."

"You can't without cowboys, either. Right now, you're shorter on cowboys than on long guns."

McAlester shifted the weight in his hands. Suddenly, he felt profound fatigue in every part of his body. More than anything else, he wanted sleep. Dreamless sleep.

"All right. We'll leave the rifles."

"You bring them yourself. When you come for these boys. Hold 'em by the barrel, away from your body."

"Agreed."

McAlester took another dozen steps up the ridge before turning around again.

"Marshal, you tell her she won." His voice carried easily across the cooling sand to the house. And, he knew, to his men on the ridge behind him. "This place is hers, and I doubt anyone will ever try to take it away from her again. But it's not worth a damn. Not a damn."

"I'll tell her."

CHAPTER 20

THEY worked side by side that first day, taking turns with the cleanup and the watching.

The work was brutally hard. Alvarez would hobble around the yard tearing down the shed or piecing together a coffin from the burnt lumber with Joe's help while Cora Diemert stood guard with the shotgun or one of the short cowboy rifles. Or she would sweep at the bloodstains that seemed impervious to her best efforts while he stood just outside the door or leaned back in a chair, his leg up and two rifles in a huge "X" across his chest.

The girls straightened the house and helped with the chores and rounded up the hens that had scattered during the long day of shooting. Some life and spirit came back to Nettie by afternoon, but Lydia remained quiet and withdrawn, especially as the burnt-wood coffin took shape.

Toward evening, Cora stood quietly with her girls and watched as Alvarez and Joe lifted what was left of Billy Shingleton's body into the makeshift coffin and set it beneath the cottonwood. When they were finished, she walked away without a word and went inside and busied herself with supper.

By the second day they both knew that the foreman had meant what he had said: the cowboys would not be back.

The boy handled the hardest part of that day's work—the digging—alone. Alvarez offered to lend a hand, but the marshal let him be when Joe just stabbed his spade harder at the iron-hard dirt without a word. Nettie came by to watch and stood there chatting softly to Pa, as she frequently did, but Joe ignored her, too. He had no words in him. Not for

Pa. Not for Billy. He dug until sweat poured into his eyes and his hands blistered, but no matter how hard he worked he couldn't get the thought of the cruelly burned, twisted thing he and Tom Alvarez had put in the charred-wood coffin out of his mind. Then he thought of the day Billy had taught him how to shoot and the secrets they had had. Secrets that no longer needed keeping.

As soon as he finished, he took Alvarez's horse out of the corral, saddled it, lashed the spade to the cantle, and rode off alone. His mother saw him and ran after him, but he dug his heels into the horse and was gone.

When he finally came riding into the yard an hour past sunset, Cora hurried outside to scold him, but words failed her as Joe calmly unsaddled the horse and handed her something very heavy wrapped in a dirty horse blanket.

"I reckon Billy would have wanted you to have this, Ma," he said. "I helped him bury it." He turned away and began giving the horse a good rubdown.

"You should leave," Tom Alvarez said the next morning. He had decided it would be his last morning on the Diemert place. The leg still hurt, but his work was ended. All he had left to do was to ride on to Las Vegas somehow and hire a wagon that might take him back to Kansas.

She stirred oatmeal and said nothing. She had fed the children already and sent them outside to look after the livestock. A strand of hair fell in her eyes and she brushed it out of the way.

"That cowboy was right, you know," he said. "This place isn't worth much. You should leave."

She lifted the pot off the stove and ladled oatmeal into two clean china bowls. "I've been thinking maybe we ought to stay. Try to make a go of it."

"That's foolish."

She looked him straight in the eye. "I suppose it is, Marshal. But we've worked for this place. And we've buried our dead here." She sat down, said grace, and ate in silence.

Alvarez finished his own breakfast before he broached the subject again. "You'll have to hire hands to look after your cattle, and the shed needs rebuilding. That'll take money."

"We'll cut back. Maybe I can sell some of the herd to a neighbor. Trade cattle for lumber and a milch cow this year. Next year the childen will be bigger, so we'll be able to tend a larger garden. We'll get by somehow."

"That's brave talk," he said, "but you have to be realistic . . ."

She looked up at him and he saw tears in her eyes. "It's not brave," she said. "It terrifies me. But our blood is in this land now. Good or bad, we've fought for this place. I can't run away from that. This family has run enough."

"You should leave," he said again halfheartedly.

Her jaw tightened and she blinked away the tears. "I won't."

He sipped at his coffee. "I know."

She turned to look out the open door. Warm yellow sunlight flooded her yard. "Well then," she said, "it's time we said some words over Billy Shingleton." She faced Alvarez and gave him something like a smile in spite of the sorrow that clearly threatened to overwhelm her. "It's hard to say good-bye to him, you know."

He watched her for a while before answering. She was a strong woman, handsome and determined. He'd never met one quite like her.

"I know that, too," was all he said, and he followed her outside.

The children stood at the foot of the tree for a long time after Cora had read the resurrection story and her favorite selections of Psalms and Alvarez had scooped the yellow dirt back into the hole. Joe twisted his hat in his hands and stared at the two graves, the old one that had been there long enough now to take on the rough contours of the ground and the color and texture of the sod, and the new one, so fresh and stark and ugly. The one he'd dug himself.

Joe closed his eyes tight against the memory of the other charred corpse the cowboys had removed by lantern-light that first night and how it had looked so much like the body they had left behind. Neither body had looked human, and Joe had recognized Billy Shingleton from size alone. Any other identifiable feature was gone.

He opened his eyes and looked at the graves again and forced such thoughts from his mind. Because he had to.

Marshal Tom Alvarez was preparing to leave: he had brought his horse around behind the house and was saddling it with some difficulty. The horse wouldn't hold still and he had trouble keeping his balance on one good leg, so finally he tethered the bay to the corral fence to keep it still. The swaybacked mule and the bull both nibbled at the grass in their pens and looked on indifferently.

Alvarez finished the saddling, untied his horse, took the reins in his teeth, and hauled himself up into the saddle, using his right hand to wrestle the splinted leg over the cantle. It pained him some, but of course he didn't let it show.

It was time to be off.

"You'll be all right, then, Mrs. Diemert?" he asked.

She brushed the stubborn wisp of hair out of her face and stared up at him.

"Yes," she said. Then she turned to her children. "Joe, go get the bags for Marshal Alvarez."

The boy turned away from the grave. He gave Alvarez a sour glance and then his mother a softer, more beseeching look.

"Please get them, Joseph."

The boy gave in. "Yes, ma'am." He put his head down and ran to the house.

"He's getting something that rightly belongs to others,

Marshal," she said. "It's the stolen money, I believe. You'll see to it that it gets back to where it belongs?"

"Mrs. Diemert . . ." He looked down on her. Tom Alvarez had made a life of doing his duty, and now for the first time in many years he wished he could ride away from it, escape it completely. The woman needed help desperately if she was going to make a go of this place, and what better help than this money to pay off the bankers and buy decent breeding stock and hire some help? What chance did a woman really have in this country without a man? Even as strong a woman as Cora Diemert . . .

The boy returned carrying the saddlebags and a small basket draped with a towel.

"There's a lunch in the basket," she said. "I trust it will hold you until you can get a decent meal in town."

"Thank you, ma'am." He took the basket and looped the handle over the saddle horn. Joe reluctantly held up the bags, but Alvarez didn't take them. Cora nudged the boy, who held them higher.

"You ought to sell the place, Mrs. Diemert," Alvarez said, ignoring the gesture. "Those cowboys we fought off may not be back, but in time there will be others. Other cowboys, maybe even other settlers like you who'll try to steal a place like this, with good water and shelter."

"There will be trying times. But I'm not selling. Or giving up. Now take this blood money with you."

"I could report that the money was never found."

"But it was. And I'll have no part of it." She nudged her son again.

Of course she was right, and of course he had his duty to do in the matter: the money would have to go back to Larned. Where it belonged. He took the heavy bags from Joe and settled them across his lap. There would be time later for strapping them down. "As you wish," he said.

"Well then," she said, giving him one of her fiercest, most manlike looks, "thank you. For everything."

He swept off the big felt hat. "And thank you, Cora, for my life!"

He nudged the big horse in the ribs with his good foot and tugged on the reins to head it west.

"Marshal, there is one thing," she called out after him. "I need a buckboard and another mule. I do have a few dollars put aside. If I give you the money, would you buy them for me in Wagon Mound and have the livery man bring them out?"

Alvarez stopped the horse and turned it around. "Why not have Joe ride along with me? He can buy them there and bring them back himself."

Cora blinked and started to say something but stopped. Her boy looked at the big man in amazement.

"He's the man of the family now," Alvarez said simply, "and it's time he started doing a man's chores."

"Yes," she said, smiling at her son. "It is."

Evening came on with glorious color, and she took her rocking chair out under the cottonwood to read her Psalms by the dying light. She would not rest until Joe returned to her, and perhaps for many nights thereafter. Fear still gnawed at her, and she knew the struggle to hold this place might, in the long run, consume her. She had lost a husband and a friend in the struggle already.

But it *was* worth fighting for. And not just because her dead were buried here. Or because the water was as good and the grass as sweet as Missouri. There was more, too. Henry, for all his faults, had seen something in this country that she'd been blind to, something she'd refused to see. Something that made a man dream big dreams. She owed it to her children to rediscover that something for them.

She read until she could no longer see, and then she rocked in the grass and listened to the breeze rustle the fat cottonwood leaves as the summer stars winked on in the velvet darkness of the sky.

If you have enjoyed this book and would like to receive details of other Walker Western titles, please write to:

Western Editor
Walker and Company
720 Fifth Avenue
New York, NY 10019